Julian Symons is primarily remembered as a master of the art of crime writing. However, in his eighty-two years he produced an enormously varied body of work. Social and military history, biography and criticism were all subjects he touched upon with remarkable success, and he held a distinguished reputation in each field.

His novels were consistently highly individual and expertly crafted, raising him above other crime writers of his day. It is for this that he was awarded various prizes, and, in 1982, named as Grand Master of the Mystery Writers of America – an honour accorded to only three other English writers before him: Graham Greene, Eric Ambler and Daphne du Maurier. He succeeded Agatha Christie as the president of Britain's Detection Club, a position he held from 1976 to 1985, and in 1990 he was awarded the Cartier Diamond Dagger from the British Crime Writers' Association for his lifetime's achievement in crime fiction.

Symons died in 1994.

BY THE SAME AUTHOR
ALL PUBLISHED BY HOUSE OF STRATUS

CRIME/SUSPENSE:

THE 31ST OF FEBRUARY
THE BELTING INHERITANCE
BLAND BEGINNING
THE BROKEN PENNY
THE COLOUR OF MURDER
THE END OF SOLOMON GRUNDY
THE GIGANTIC SHADOW
THE IMMATERIAL MURDER CASE
THE KILLING OF FRANCIE LAKE
A MAN CALLED JONES
THE MAN WHO KILLED HIMSELF
THE MAN WHO LOST HIS WIFE
THE MAN WHOSE DREAMS CAME TRUE
THE NARROWING CIRCLE
THE PAPER CHASE
THE PLAYERS AND THE GAME
THE PLOT AGAINST ROGER RIDER
A THREE-PIPE PROBLEM

HISTORY/CRITICISM:

BULLER'S CAMPAIGN
THE TELL-TALE HEART: THE LIFE AND
    WORKS OF EDGAR ALLEN POE
ENGLAND'S PRIDE
THE GENERAL STRIKE
HORATIO BOTTOMLEY
THE THIRTIES
THOMAS CARLYLE

The Progress of a Crime

Julian Symons

HOUSE OF
STRATUS

This edition published in 2001 by House of Stratus, an imprint of
Stratus Holdings plc, 24c Old Burlington Street, London, W1X 1RL, UK.
Also at: Suite 210, 1270 Avenue of the Americas, New York, NY 10020, USA

www.houseofstratus.com

Typeset, printed and bound by House of Stratus.

A catalogue record for this book is available from the British Library
and The Library of Congress

ISBN 1-84232-921-9

FOR KATE FULLER

INTRODUCTION

The French call a typewriter *une machine á ècrire*. It is a description that could well be applied to Julian Symons, except the writing he produced had nothing about it smelling of the mechanical. The greater part of his life was devoted to putting pen to paper. Appearing in 1938, his first book was a volume of poetry, *Confusions About X*. In 1996, after his death, there came his final crime novel, *A Sort of Virtue* (written even though he knew he was under sentence from an inoperable cancer) beautifully embodying the painful come-by lesson that it is possible to achieve at least a degree of good in life.

His crime fiction put him most noticeably into the public eye, but he wrote in many forms: biographies, a memorable piece of autobiography (*Notes from Another Country*), poetry, social history, literary criticism coupled with year-on-year reviewing and two volumes of military history, and one string thread runs through it all. Everywhere there is a hatred of hypocrisy, hatred even when it aroused the delighted fascination with which he chronicled the siren schemes of that notorious jingoist swindler, Horatio Bottomley, both in his biography of the man and fictionally in *The Paper Chase* and *The Killing of Francie Lake*.

That hatred, however, was not a spew but a well-spring. It lay behind what he wrote and gave it force, yet it was always tempered by a need to speak the truth. Whether he was writing about people as fiction or as fact, if he had a low opinion of them he simply told the truth as he saw it, no more and no less.

This adherence to truth fills his novels with images of the mask. Often it is the mask of hypocrisy. When, as in *Death's Darkest Face* or *Something Like a Love Affair*, he chose to use a plot of dazzling legerdemain, the masks of cunning are startlingly ripped away.

The masks he ripped off most effectively were perhaps those which people put on their true faces when sex was in the air or under the exterior. 'Lift the stone, and sex crawls out from under,' says a character in that relentless hunt for truth, *The Progress of a Crime*, a book that achieved the rare feat for a British author, winning Symons the US Edgar Allen Poe Award.

Julian was indeed something of a pioneer in the fifties and sixties bringing into the almost sexless world of the detective story the truths of sexual situations. 'To exclude realism of description and language from the crime novel' he writes in *Critical Occasions*, 'is almost to prevent its practitioners from attempting any serious work.' And then the need to unmask deep-hidden secrecies of every sort was almost as necessary at the end of his crime-writing life as it had been at the beginning. Not for nothing was his last book subtitled *A Political Thriller.*

H R F Keating
London, 2001

Chapter One

Hugh Bennett had lunch that day as usual in Giuseppe's, which was the only good place to eat near the office. Good, that is, and cheap. The wages that the *Gazette* paid its staff made the second consideration important. He was half-way through his spaghetti when Clare Cavendish came in with Michael Baker. Clare looked at the menu with distaste.

"The same old stuff. Spaghetti, ravioli, fruit salad. I'm so sick of it."

Michael Baker, whom nobody ever called Mike, fingered his bow tie. "Getting you down, dear?"

"And it's so bad for my figure." Clare's face had a sulky prettiness, spoiled by a bad complexion, but her figure was excellent, tall and slim. She crumbled a piece of bread in her fingers as she talked in petulant spurts. "Went out to see some ghastly old creature in Bradley this morning. Ninety-eight today. Three-quarters deaf, almost blind, crippled with arthritis. Said she hoped to live another ten years, there was so much to live for. Christ." Clare had made several bread pellets, which she formed into the letter C.

"It really is too much," Michael said, in his slightly fluting voice. "I don't know what old Lane's up to lately. I mean, *either* I'm the dramatic critic *or* I can handle police courts and that stuff. I've had the dreariest morning, stealing bicycles and indecent exposure, hardly a paragraph in the lot. Old Prothero was rather funny, though, with one chap... " He wove spaghetti dextrously round his fork and told them exactly how funny old Prothero, the magistrate, had been.

Hugh Bennett sat and ate and listened. He was twenty-two years old, and had been on the *Gazette* for eighteen months, which was quite long enough to understand that Clare and Michael did not mean exactly what they said. They knew perfectly well that on a local paper like the *Gazette* the dramatic critic must double and even treble up on other jobs, and that the writer of the woman's page must expect to be sent out on human interest stories. They griped because they wanted to go to London, to work on one of the nationals. But did those who griped ever get there? Now Michael was astride his high aesthetic horse.

"I do think Tynan's a bit much, don't you? On again about Brecht last week, hardly a word to say about the new plays, got rid of them in half a dozen lines. I mean, I really should think readers are getting a bit sick of it."

Clare was not interested in Tynan, but she had some very positive views about women columnists, and spent some time in telling them about the shortcomings of Veronica Papworth and Anne Scott-James. It was very much like twenty other lunches they had had together, with the smell of pipe-dream perhaps stronger than usual. As they walked back to the office Clare asked, "What are you doing this afternoon, Hugh?"

"Diary. Valuation court at Far Wether."

"Poor you."

"Far Wether," Michael said. "Let me think. Something happened a couple of weeks ago at Far Wether. Madge Gilroy sent in a story about it. Some sort of Teddy-boy row, might be worth looking up since you've got to go out there."

Hugh nodded his thanks. He did not want to go out to Far Wether, and when they got back to the office he said hopefully to Lane, "Anything interesting come in?"

Lane grinned at him, exposing a few yellow fangs. He was a hard-bitten provincial newspaper veteran in his early fifties, the sort of man who sits in his shirtsleeves all day and has sandwiches and a glass of milk sent in to the office for lunch. Clare and Michael treated Lane as a joke, but to Hugh he was still a slightly awesome figure, a man who had, as he was fond of saying, printer's ink in his veins instead of blood.

"It's the valuation court for you, Hughie boy. Good training."

"For what?"

"For attending more valuation courts," Michael said.

"Elizabeth Eglington is opening a new store in Bank Street," Lane said to him. "Go and see her, try to get her to talk about her screen ambitions, what she thinks of our great city, does she like the new traffic roundabout in the square. She may fall for your manly charm."

Michael looked offended. Hugh went over and turned the pages of the back issues. He found the story tucked away on page six among the "News From the Districts" in a fortnight-old paper.

HOOLIGANISM AT FAR WETHER DANCE

A group of youths caused trouble last Saturday at a fund-raising dance for the Far Wether Cricket Club held in the Parish Hall. It is said that they came to the village on motorbikes, threw bottles on the dance floor and pestered several girls who did not want to dance with them. Mr James Corby, a local resident, who was MC at the dance, said: "I did not like their looks when they came in, but of course our dances are open to anybody who buys a ticket. When they got out of hand I asked them to leave, and after a little persuasion they did so." Other local residents said that Mr Corby had thrown out bodily the two worst members of the gang. As they drove away one of them shouted, "We'll be back." Mr

Corby, however, is confident that there will be no further trouble.

He finished reading the story and asked, "Do you want me this evening?"

Lane was in the process of lighting a small cigar. He looked at Bennett above the smoke.

"It's Guy Fawkes Night and you want to let off your golden rain, is that it?"

"I thought I'd see if there was any follow-up on this."

Lane read the story and used a four-letter word. Clare showed no sign of having heard it, but the corners of her mouth turned down a little more disdainfully, even, than usual. Lane slapped the paper and repeated the word. "But if you're going to stay out in Far Wether I'll tell you what you *can* do. They have a real do there on November the fifth, don't burn Guy Fawkes in effigy but burn Squire Oldmeadow instead. Ever heard of him?" Hugh Bennett shook his head. "He was one of the bad old squires in the good old days, ground down the serfs and raped their daughters and that sort of caper. There's a legend that some local hero named Francis Drake up and killed the wicked squire because Squire had wronged his sister."

" I don't believe it. You've made it all up."

"Want to brush up on your local history, my lad." Lane had got the cigar going well. Smoke dimmed the outline of his grizzled head. "They burn the old squire out in Far Wether. Fact. Do a piece on it."

That was how it began.

Chapter Two

Far Wether was nearly twelve miles to the south-west of the city, too near for complete independence yet too far to count as a suburb. It was in an area usually covered by Madge Gilroy, who lived in the district and worked for the *Gazette* part-time. It was because Madge had influenza that Hugh Bennett found himself travelling out in a bus through Felting and High Oaks, and reading *Anna of the Five Towns* on the way. Arnold Bennett was the writer that Hugh most admired, envying his unfussy directness, his brisk humanitarianism, his eager appetite for life. He seemed a proof that a novelist's virtues can also be those of a journalist, and Hugh Bennett often felt warmed by the fact that he shared a surname with Arnold. A slight euphoria stayed with him as he entered the newish square red-brick council offices on the edge of the village, in which the court was being held.

Attendance at a valuation court is perhaps the dullest of the many dull jobs a young provincial journalist can have. A magistrate's court may have its saving pawky humour, a local council meeting its brief delicious flare of excitement as opposed personalities meet head-on, but the tedium of a valuation court is invariable. On this grey November afternoon the court was concerned chiefly with an appeal against his rating valuation made by a man who lived in a row of semi-detached houses just outside Far Wether. This particular house, unlike its fellows, had a garage, and so was rated at £32 a year, whereas they were rated at £29. Its owner appealed on the ground that if he had owned a car (which in fact he did not) he could not have used the garage because the only access to it was by a lane at the back of his house, and this lane was too narrow to permit the passage of a car.

But was this in fact the case? The council's surveyor produced plans, the house-owner disputed them, the surveyor agreed that the lane might perhaps not be wide enough to accommodate a car. Was this surrender? By no means. Triumphantly the surveyor suggested that it would be perfectly possible to take a bubble car or a scooter along the lane. Vain for the house-owner to protest that he had no wish to buy a bubble car, and considered scooters extremely unsafe. Two-thirds of his case was adjudged lost and, after a discussion lasting an hour and a half, his rating was reduced from £32 to £31 a year.

Two other reporters from local papers, both of them weeklies, sat at the little table provided for the press. One wrote half a dozen personal letters, the other read a book by Graham Greene. Hugh would have liked to return to *Anna of the Five Towns,* but he remembered a maxim that he had read somewhere in Arnold, that all material was useful to a writer. This material, then, must somehow be useful too. By half-past five, when the court finished, he felt less sure about this.

Far Wether consisted of one long, straggling street with houses and shops placed randomly along it, opening out into a large and pretty village green. Houses were dotted round this green and on the edge of it stood the local pub, the Dog and Duck. He went into this pub, ordered a pint of beer, and asked what time the bonfire would be starting.

" 'Bout half an hour's time," the landlord said. "Isn't that right, Mr Corby?"

"Six-fifteen on the dot," said Mr Corby. "All laid on. Be trouble if Joe Pickett's late." He was a big man, a very big man, rising some three inches above Bennett's six feet, and broad into the bargain. He had a fleshy face with a big, pushing nose and bright, inquisitive eyes. A jovial, smiling man, but one to keep the right side of, Hugh Bennett thought, perhaps a bit of a Squire Oldmeadow in his way. As if to confirm his thoughts Mr Corby rapped out quite sharply: "Come down for the bonfire? Worth seeing."

"I'm from the *Gazette*. My name's Bennett. I've just been covering the valuation court, and thought I'd stay on for a bit."

Mr Corby's potential frown changed to an actual smile. "Glad to have you. George, give the young man a drink. Yes, we put on a pretty good show for a little village. Burn the old squire in effigy. You've heard of Squire Oldmeadow?"

"Of course."

"Ha," said Mr Corby, slightly disappointed. "He was a real bad 'un. Can't do with 'em like that in these days, can we, Rogers?" he barked to a man at the other end of the bar.

The man, old and weather-beaten, shook his head.

"Not by no means, Mr Corby."

"Certainly can't. Have a drink."

"Thankee, Mr Corby. I won't say no to a half of bitter."

"Can't understand you newspaper chaps." Mr Corby roasted his big behind in front of the fire. "Fill up the paper with all kinds of stuff nobody wants to read, and often miss what's right under your noses. The *Gazette*, now, that's a local paper – "

"An independent paper." Hugh Bennett could not quite keep the pride out of his voice. "And we're really competing with the nationals in this area. We try to give a full coverage of national and local news."

"Ha," Mr Corby said again, expressively. He was obviously a man not much given to argument. "More news from the districts, that's what people want to read. Keep up local tradition. 'Field and Farm,' now, that's a good column, I enjoy that."

"We had a piece about Far Wether a week or two back. About a little trouble you had here."

"Gang of young hooligans. Told them to mind their manners and then said, 'We don't want your type here thank you very much, prefer your room to your company.' When they still wouldn't move I used a little gentle persuasion."

"They said they'd come back. You don't think that's likely?

The big man threw back his head and laughed. The laughter, picked up by others, rippled through the bar, the militant laughter of those protected by beer and warmth.

"They won't come back," said a bottle-nosed farmer wearing a big check muffler. "Jim here could take on three of them with one hand behind his back. They had enough the first time."

The door opened, and a little man with his head fixed as it seemed permanently on one side, his general look one of idiot cunning, came in. "Fire's a beauty, Mr Corby."

"Good man, Joe. Have a pint. George, bring out the Squire."

While Joe Pickett cocked his head sideways over beer, the landlord brought out from somewhere at the back a rather over life-size stuffed figure, wearing a billycock hat and dressed in nankeen jacket and leggings, and heavy boots. The face had been painted on canvas, and wore a look of red-cheeked moustachioed fury. Mr Corby affectionately slapped the figure on the shoulder.

"There he is. Have him made up exactly according to the clothes he wore in an old print I've got at home. Costs more than a tenner every year. See what I mean, Bennett, about the importance of local traditions? Got to keep 'em up. Are we all ready?"

The ceremony that followed was conducted with perfect seriousness. Four men carried the squire on their shoulders, Mr Corby and the bottle-nosed farmer at the front, and lopsided Joe Pickett with a tall, thin, lugubrious man at the rear. As they came out of the pub and turned on to the green, boys with torches met them and surrounded the procession. In the middle of the green figures were visible round a bonfire, and towards this bonfire the group from the pub steadily moved. Once Corby stumbled over a hillock and cursed. Somebody threw a cracker under Hugh Bennett's feet, where it snapped at him furiously.

The people round the fire, most of them men and children, gave a scattered cheer as the squire reached them and was placed upright on the grass, with Mr Corby's arm round his shoulders. A rocket sizzled skyward and burst into a flower of stars. Mr Corby's voice roared out.

"Who are we burning here tonight?"

The reply came, ragged but enthusiastic. "We burn Squire Oldmeadow, who lived here in the Manor House."

"Why do we burn him?"

"He was a bad squire. He cheated those who trusted in him."

"How did he cheat you?"

"He stole our land and our women."

"And what was his end?"

"He was killed in fair fight by the freeman Francis Drake."

"Which of you tonight will be Francis Drake?" shouted bull-voiced Corby.

"I will." Lopsided Joe Pickett came forward.

"Then, Francis Drake, I pass to you this effigy of Squire Oldmeadow. Make sure that he is well and truly burned."

The effigy was evidently fairly heavy. Joe Pickett staggered slightly as he lifted it to his shoulder. Then he took two steps forward towards the fire, and threw the figure. It landed almost in the heart of the bonfire. There was another cheer.

Mr Corby peered round and saw Hugh Bennett. "How about that, eh?"

"Very interesting."

"Someone's got to keep up the old customs. Though they don't take the interest they did."

"Who lives in the Manor House now?"

Mr Corby stared hard at him. "I do."

Faintly, in the distance, Hugh Bennett heard the hum of motorcycles.

Chapter Three

The sound became louder, developed to a roar. Suddenly half a dozen searchlights were focused from the road by the green on to the scene beside the bonfire. The searchlights went out, the engines of the motorcycles were cut off. This stopping of the engines gave some curious quality to the scene, a quality that made Bennett shiver. It was not silence, for beside him the bonfire blazed and crackled, and all around children were waving sparklers and golden rain. A voice beside him said, "I want a light. Have you got a light? Can you light these?"

He looked down at a small dark girl who held half a dozen fireworks. "Which one?"

"All of them."

"Not all at once."

"Yes – *all at once.* It's my own firework show."

"I'll light two, one for each hand. Put the rest in your pocket." A firework banged loudly, so near him that he almost dropped the box of matches he had taken out. The whole scene was dipped in green light.

Nearby, somebody said, "That's him."

The fireworks were alight. He gave them to the little girl, turned, and saw a youth, pale-faced and slim, pointing. The youth's finger pointed beyond him to where Corby stood lighting a catherine wheel tied to a post.

Another voice said, "Now." Then a ragged volley of lighted fireworks was thrown at Corby. A Roman candle threw up its blobs of fire beside his feet, a flying torpedo whizzed round his head, a mine of serpents struck his coat and exploded almost in his face. Corby stood still for a moment, bewildered, then roared with anger and rushed forward. As he did so his attackers – there were at least three or four of them, ranged roughly in a semi-circle – retreated, and lighted and threw more fireworks. The scene, in the flare of green fire, was like a parody of a bullfight, as Corby rushed forwards and sideways.

"They'll never come back," one of the boys called in a falsetto voice. "They'll never come back."

Now Corby knew who his assailants were, but he did not call for help. One of the youths slipped in the mud and almost fell, and in an instant the big man was on him. The disturbance had been noticed by only a few people standing on this side of the fire, but Bennett felt that he should take some part in it. He put one hand on the shoulder of the youth beside him, the one who had pointed, and began to say something. The hand was struck away. He put his arms round the youth, and felt something hard in his pocket. Then the other pulled himself free and stumbled over the little girl whose fireworks Bennett had lighted. They went down together, the little girl crying out something. Hugh Bennett lunged for the youth but missed him. He ran away towards Corby. The green flare went out.

After that, several things seemed to happen simultaneously. He helped the little girl up, and tried to stop her crying. A voice shouted, "Get him, King." Another voice, one that he had heard before – was it Joe Pickett's? – cried out, "You stop that, now. I'm calling the police." Another still, and this he knew to be Corby's, shouted, "Put that knife down."

There followed a cry, a long wailing animal cry. Dark figures ran over the green. There was the sound of motor-cycles starting up and roaring away down the road. And after that, in spite of the fire's crackle and the spit and bang of fireworks, there was what, to Hugh Bennett, seemed very much like silence.

"What's your name?" he said to the girl.

"Maureen Dyer. My coat's dirty. That man pushed me over. And I've dropped my yellow dragons."

"Yellow dragons? Oh, I see." He groped in the muddy grass, found thin, long shapes. "They're a bit wet, but perhaps they'll still light. Let's see."

"He was a horrible man," the girl said, as he put a match to the touch-paper.

"Wasn't he? I'm afraid this won't – " A spurt of flame came from the firework. "Oh yes, it will. Here you are. I've got some of the others too."

She waved the yellow dragon at him. "I'm going to find Mummy."

Even before she merged with the other grotesques who danced and played in the bonfire's flame, he had been uneasily aware of something going on in the place from which that cry had come. Voices called confusedly, a group of people could be seen moving about, busy and apparently purposeless. He moved over, and was stopped by somebody who seemed to be grinning up into his face. It was Joe Pickett.

"Where's Doctor Mackintosh? Oh, you're the reporter."

"What's the matter?"

"I think Mr Corby's had a fit or something." He moved away, calling out "Dr. Mackintosh".

A few yards farther, and he was with a dozen people who stood about something lying on the ground. "It's those boys out from the city on their bikes," a woman said.

"What's happened?"

Nobody answered. A man in a duffle coat said, "Mind you, Corby asked for it. The way he threw them out that night was rough, very rough."

13

"And why should they come pestering our girls?" the woman asked.

"What's happened?" Hugh Bennett asked again.

"Couple of these young toughs set on to Corby, knocked him out," duffle coat replied. "He'll be all right in a couple of minutes."

"Did you see it?"

"Too dark to see much. Here's the doctor."

Doctor Mackintosh proved to be the tall, lugubrious man who had helped to carry Squire Oldmeadow. Joe Pickett was with him. "Don't crowd round now," the doctor said rather pettishly. "Please don't crowd round."

By the torch in Pickett's hand it was possible to see a figure lying still, covered by an overcoat or rug. The doctor knelt by him and then spoke again, in a voice sharp but no longer pettish. "Joe."

"Yes, Doctor."

"Run to the Dog and Duck and ask George to ring for an ambulance. It's urgent."

"Yes, Doctor. Is he bad?"

"He's badly hurt. Some of you help me lift him."

Bennett was one of those who helped to carry the big man back to the pub from which, so recently, they had brought Squire Oldmeadow. They took him into the back parlour and as they put him down on a sofa, Bennett saw the dark mark on his tweed overcoat. The landlord came in.

"I've phoned the hospital. Is there anything else?"

"Bandages," the doctor said. He had the overcoat off, and was undoing Corby's jacket and waistcoat.

"Bless me, he looks bad. Is it an accident?"

"He's been stabbed. More than once, I think." The doctor's hands were stained red.

"Stabbed," Hugh Bennett exclaimed.

"By one of those young thugs from the city." He spoke as though the reporter were in some way responsible.

Hugh looked at the red face that was now the colour of dough and at the probing nose, now a chalky promontory.

"You mean – "

"I mean I'm doing what I can for him, but that's nothing at all." At that moment Corby opened his eyes and looked about. The doctor spoke gently. "Easy does it, Jim. Don't move."

Corby opened his mouth as if to speak. Blood gushed from his mouth and nose. His eyes closed again. Bennett turned away his head.

"I'd like to wash my hands, George," Doctor Mackintosh said.

" Is he gone, Doctor?"

" Yes," the doctor said. "He's dead."

Chapter Four

The hour that followed was perhaps the most confused period of time in Hugh Bennett's life. It was vitally important for him to get back to the *Gazette* office as quickly as possible, so that he could write his story, yet it was at the same time essential that he should wait for the police to arrive, and get an idea of what sort of man Corby was. He rang up from the pub and told Lane, who was still in the office, what had happened.

"You really stepped in it today, didn't you? When can you get back?"

"I want to get some background stuff on Corby. I ought to talk to Joe Buckley, he's the constable round here. And probably it would be a good thing to go over and see Madge. I shall be a couple of hours, maybe more."

" – Madge," Lane said. "She won't tell you anything. And – Buckley, too, while you're about it. He won't know half as much as you do. I tell you what you do. Get what you can on Corby, go and see Mrs C if there is one, then get back here by eight-fifteen. Take a taxi."

"A taxi?" he said incredulously.

"It'll come out of linage," Lane said, and laughed.

In his excitement he had forgotten about the linage, but he could understand Lane's concern, since he held the linage for the paper. This meant that, when Hugh got back, he would telephone all the national dailies one by one, dressing up the story a bit differently for each of them. Then he would telephone the news agencies. Sometime in between telephone calls he would write his *Gazette* story, but from the cash point of view the linage was the thing. Even after Lane had taken his whack out of it the story would be worth – what? At least twenty-five pounds, possibly nearer fifty. Hugh Bennett sighed. It occurred to him, not for the first time, that the life of a provincial reporter was extraordinarily unromantic.

Mrs Corby was a thin-nosed grey woman who talked to him composedly, rather as if her husband had broken a leg and was bound to be incapacitated for a few weeks. Three or four times she referred to him in the present tense, and then corrected herself with no sign of emotion. Bennett still felt a little uneasy and ashamed when met by tears, and was grateful for her calm. He made notes in an abbreviated long-hand scrawl:

James C. Age 52. Local res. Partner in timber merchants, C and Jenkins. Liked in village??? says no enemies. V strong, had been amateur boxer. Married 20 years, no family. Bt. Manor Ho. 1946…

He put down a page of such notes, then checked them by talking to people in the pub. As he expected, Corby had not been greatly liked in Far Wether. Through the mist of praise that surrounds anybody recently dead, criticism could be discerned – he had done a lot for the village, mark you, never minded what he did or how much trouble he took, but he had taken too much on himself, always wanted to be number one. But the pub regulars didn't want to talk about Corby so much as about the youths, the destroyers who had roared in on their motorbikes and killed a man and roared away again. Joe Pickett confidently maintained that they were the boys who had come to the dance, he would recognise them anywhere.

"Don't be such a bloody fool, man," said duffle coat, whose name turned out to be Morgan. "It was dark, wasn't it? How could you see a bloody thing?"

"I saw enough," Pickett said obstinately. "I'd have known them anywhere. Recognised their voices too, some of 'em."

"And what did they say?"

"There was two of 'em on to him, and they was flashing their knives."

The tall doctor came in and stood listening. "Save it for the police, Joe," he said to Pickett. "You do your talking to them, they'll want to hear it. In the meantime, the less said the better."

Joe Pickett thrust out his lower lip, but said nothing. Conversation died as the doctor glared round at them.

"Can you say anything about the cause of death?" Hugh Bennett asked.

"You saw he'd been stabbed, didn't you? Nothing more to say. There's been enough trouble here tonight, talk will only make more."

He was back just after eight-fifteen. The *Gazette's* main entrance was in the High Street, a bit of red-brick Victorian Gothic, but the reporters always used the dingy back way in through Cressiter Lane. He squeezed past great rolls of paper and went up an iron staircase. A lamp of low wattage shone dimly on the tiled walls, making the corridor look more than usually like the entrance to a public lavatory. He passed *Editor Private* and *Gentlemen* and went in the door that said *Reporters' Room.*

"Well, cock," Lane said, "got your story written?"

The way to treat Lane, he knew, was to answer bullying joviality with bullying joviality, to say that if he was in such a hurry he could write the story himself. Somehow, though, he stood too much in awe of Lane to say anything like that. So now he made some equivocal, some vaguely placatory reply, which indicated his sorrow that he hadn't performed the impossibility of writing the story on the way back in the taxi.

"Pull your finger out and get to it. The *Express* first. For them no sex angle."

"There isn't one."

"There's always a sex angle. Lift the stone and sex crawls out from under. Then the *Mail, Mirror, Banner, Chronicle, Herald.* Five hundred words each. Then the *Telegraph* and *The Times,* couple of hundred each. Then the agencies. All right?"

"What shall I do for us?"

Lane was smoking another of his small cigars. He looked over the top of it like a wild pig about to charge. "A thousand."

"With a by-line?"

The glare of the pig's little eyes grew dangerous, then creases showed round them. "With a by-line. Do the *Express* and *Mail* and I'll give a hand with the others myself."

It was half-past eleven when they had finished, and he felt limp. There was a rule against bringing drink into the office, but Lane unlocked a drawer of his desk, and produced a bottle of whisky. Michael had come in after watching a local amateur dramatic society perform *The Years Between,* and he shared in the whisky that Lane poured into tooth-glasses.

"Here's to journalism, and to the blooding of this young feller-me-lad," he said. "You get it easy here, sitting on your backsides half the day. This is just a glimpse of what work's like. When I was on the *Express* before the war, every day we used to… "

Michael made a face as he sipped his whisky. He and Clare and one or two of the others said that Lane had never worked on a London paper in his life, but Hugh Bennett did not believe them. The two of them left at about midnight, with Lane's final instructions ringing in his ear about telephoning the BBC and ITA regional offices in the morning. "And don't forget the follow-ups for the news agencies," he had shouted as they were going down the stairs.

It had been a deeply significant evening, and the word "blooding" seemed to have its special rightness, for he really did feel as, he imagined, the young boy must feel who is blooded after seeing the killing of his first fox. As they walked through the city's deserted centre to the flat in Pile Street that he shared with Michael Baker, he could not understand why Michael also was not excited. Instead, he talked about a young girl in the play.

"Her name's Jill Gardner. I talked to her afterwards, took her out for a cup of coffee. She can't act, but she's a poppet, a perfect poppet."

Michael had a particular terminology for girls. He divided those who interested him into mares and poppets. A mare, according to Michael, was a high-stepping, high-class, altogether superior and mettlesome young creature, hard to get and inclined to demand a great deal of money and attention when got, but really well worth the trouble and expense. A poppet, on the other hand, would be in appearance much softer and more pneumatic, a snub-nosed blonde perhaps or a rather lush, sprawlingly friendly big girl. A poppet wouldn't expect to be taken to a good restaurant, or to occupy the most expensive seats at the cinema. Poppets were for every day, Michael would say, mares were an occasional weekend treat. The great majority of women who were not mares or poppets, including all women over thirty, Michael classified as cows or bitches.

With an effort, he dragged back his mind from dreams of fame. "Does that mean you want me out of the flat tomorrow night?"

"I don't work that fast." But Michael was pleased. "I told you I'd only taken her out for a cup of coffee. But she's coming round tomorrow evening. You ought to meet her."

The flat was above a greengrocer's shop. It contained a living-room, a bedroom with two single beds, a bathroom and a kitchenette, and it was cheap. It was because there was only one bedroom that Hugh had to be out of the way when Michael entertained his poppets and mares.

He was brushing his teeth when Michael said something about Far Wether. "What? What's that?"

Michael, torso bare, was washing. "I said it's only money. Don't think it's anything else."

"I don't know what you mean."

Michael's long, thin, weakly handsome face was serious. "Don't start thinking it's a golden chance for the boy reporter. It's just a chance to make money on the linage. Very nice too."

"Do you think the nationals will send people down?"

Michael rubbed his back with a loofah. "Very unlikely. They'll leave it to their stringers down here. And don't expect Grayling to fall on your neck and give you an Oscar." He imitated the editor's slightly squeaky voice. "The *Gazette* is a family paper, Bennett, this is not the sort of story we want to make a big feature. Now there's a very interesting story here about an old lady of a hundred and fourteen who's watched her first television programme and says it isn't as good as the magic lantern. Will you go out and cover that, please?"

They both laughed. But before he went to sleep that night Hugh Bennett indulged himself in a fantasy about a London editor reading the *Gazette* story, calling in his secretary, and saying: "Send a note to this young man Hugh Bennett. Say I've read his piece and ask if he can make it convenient to call in and see me sometime during the next week." Before the interview could take place he fell asleep.

Chapter Five

The story was read by night editors and news editors, and most of them found it interesting up to a point. They liked the Guy Fawkes aspect and the bit about Squire Oldmeadow, but were rather disappointed by the fact that it was a killing apparently more or less unintended, carried out by a gang of boys. Several of the papers rang up Mrs Corby, whose unemotional and, as it seemed on the telephone, almost uninterested, reaction didn't encourage them. It was a front-page story for one or two of them, but not a story which seemed likely to have any interesting follow-up. For a heading, they all used variations on the obvious theme of "The Guy Fawkes Murder."

In the *Banner* the story was featured prominently, but on an inside page, under the heading "Death Strikes at Guy Fawkes Party." The story came up for discussion at the Friday morning conference.

"It's got some 1-1-life in it, this one," said the little news editor. "Squire of v-village, bonfire night, burning in effigy. A f-features man could make something of it. Someone like George Grady."

The features editor countered quickly. "George is pretty busy the next couple of days, covering the Old Tymes Toy Show and the Guided Weapons Conference."

"It needn't be George," the news editor said. "After all, this is crime. It could be F-Fairfield."

They both looked at Edgar Crawley, who sat at the head of the table with a neutral expression. Edgar Crawley was editor of the *Banner,* but he was something more than that, he was a kind of pipeline to the *Banner's* proprietor, Lord Brackman.

Edgar Crawley was not at all the kind of editor about whom Hugh Bennett had been dreaming. He had won a scholarship from a grammar school to Oxford, and there had taken a first in history. He had written a small book on the Congress of Vienna while in his early twenties, and had occupied a fairly important post in the COI during the war. He had come to the attention of Lord Brackman by an article in which he suggested ways of forging trade links between Britain and the Soviet Union after the war. This was a theme dear at that time to Lord Brackman's heart, and Crawley moved from writing pamphlets for the COI to writing leaders for the *Banner.* Few people had all the qualities required for successful leader-writing on the *Banner,* the mental and verbal flexibility, the moral indignation quickly assumed and as quickly cast aside in favour of sheer down-to-earth commonsensical practicality, the ability to condescend towards experts in twenty different areas of commerce, politics and art. Lord Brackman always read the leaders in the *Banner* with great attention, and although perhaps he could not have written them himself, knew perfectly what he wanted them to say. He had recognised in Edgar Crawley a man almost invariably capable of saying it.

That had been several years ago, years in which Crawley had moved onwards and upwards. He had learned to smile a great deal, with his lips closed, but it was a long time since anybody had heard him laugh. The fishlike tranquillity of his youth had markedly increased with the years, so that now there was something positively glaucous about the glances he darted from side to side of the table behind his thickly pebbled glasses. He spoke, mildly as always, tapping a paper that had used the story on its front page.

"Burning in effigy and the village squire seem to be pretty well covered here. We don't want to do it a day later, do we?"

The news editor flinched a little. "Of c-course not."

"Is there another angle? Another way we can keep it going tomorrow, perhaps over the weekend?"

"Juvenile delinquency," the features editor said a little hesitantly. "I suppose you could say a thing like this spotlights the whole problem, these boys roaring in, killing somebody, roaring out again."

Crawley's smile was well in place. "Juvenile delinquency is always with us. And then we can't be sure that they were juvenile delinquents, can we? For all we know, these young people may be in their late twenties."

"You're right," said the features editor in a manly, independent way – rather as though he had been saying defiantly that Crawley was wrong. "You're perfectly right."

"We see what comes in as a follow-up from this local reporter, then, and treat it accordingly. Is that agreed?" That was agreed.

It was four o'clock that afternoon when Edgar Crawley picked up one of his telephones and heard Lord Brackman's voice, a voice deep and thick as treacle, with a clearing of the throat perpetually incipient in it. "Corby," the voice said. "Why on an inside page?"

One of Edgar Crawley's assets was his ability to remember names and identify them with stories. It was said of him that he could look at the news pages for ten minutes and identify every name and every story in them hours later. So he now had no difficulty in linking Corby with the Guy Fawkes murder, although he had been more commonly referred to as the Squire of Far Wether. Nevertheless, he now said interrogatively, "Corby?" This was a strategic move, designed to avoid answering an awkward question, and it succeeded.

"Edgar." Lord Brackman very nearly cleared his throat, and his choked voice took on a curious whining note. "I get the best journalists and I don't interfere with them. I don't tell them what to do, you know that. But this is a front-page story, Edgar."

"Yes." Crawley's voice expressed neither agreement nor disapproval. He amplified that single syllable by saying, "Yes, Brack." This was the name by which Lord Brackman, a democrat, liked to be known to his staff.

"It's a big story, Edgar," Lord Brackman said. "One with life in it. And shall I tell you why? Because it spotlights juvenile delinquency, Edgar, it really brings that out under the arclights, my boy, out into the forum of public opinion. That's a terrible thing, juvenile delinquency. It's sapping the whole foundations of British life." Lord Brackman's tone changed suddenly, the whine turned sharp. "What are you doing about it? What's in hand?"

"We hadn't quite decided. I think Frank Fairfield."

"Frank is the best crime man in Fleet Street, but can he get the *humanity*? This is a human story. How did they get to be like this, these young boys, what sort of homes did they come from, *why* did they do it? Why, Edgar, why?"

Crawley did not attempt to answer this rhetorical question, but merely said, "I think Frank can handle that side of it, Brack. If not, we'll send a features man down."

"You've confidence in Frank for a thing like this?"

It was against Crawley's practice, one might almost say against his principles, ever to commit himself to such an expression of confidence. But there was no help for it. "Yes."

"That's all I want to know, Edgar." Lord Brackman's voice changed again, taking on a high singing note expressive of human optimism. "If you've got confidence in Frank, that's good enough for me. I trust my boys, I don't tell them what to do or who's the best man for a job. G'bye, Edgar."

"Goodbye, Brack."

Edgar Crawley sat for a few seconds after he had replaced the receiver in its cradle, looking out from his small office into the room beyond, the big room in which the features men and the star reporters and the secretaries sat in one conglomerate noisy heap, chattering away with their mouths on telephones or with their fingers on typewriters. Was he regretting the life he had chosen with its endless necessary betrayals of the personality, was he thinking back to that book on the Congress of Vienna written in the sunlit simplicity of youth? These are romantic notions, and in Crawley's mind there was no room for such luxuries. He asked his secretary to see if the news and features editors could spare him a few minutes. When he faced them he was his impersonal fishlike self.

"I think you said this morning that Frank Fairfield was free," he said to the news editor.

The features editor knew what was coming, and wondered only why he had been called in to the office. The news editor had been with the *Banner* only a few months, and was less percipient. "He's got one or two things on, but nothing very important."

"Could he go down and cover this Guy Fawkes murder?"

"B-but I thought – "

"There's a way we could do it that would make it a front-page story," Crawley said in his gentle voice.

"Supposing we used the case to emphasise the theme of juvenile delinquency. Find out who these thugs are, why they did it, what sort of homes they came from, and so on."

The news editor looked at the features editor, and waited for him to say that this had been his own idea. The features editor did nothing of the sort. He nodded thoughtfully, and said, "I see that. But is Frank just the man for it?"

"If he's briefed properly, I think yes." Crawley put the tips of his fingers together as though he were expounding a thesis. "The way to tackle this, as I see it, is to play up both the mystery and the human interest angles. If we need to send down someone from features we will. In the meantime Frank can nose round as usual, talk to the local police and so on – he's pretty good at that. This local boy who was on the spot, Bennett, what paper does he work for, would it be the *Gazette?* Frank just might get some leads from him. Will you two brief Frank together?"

The news editor found it impossible to stay silent. "Th-this is exactly what we were talking about this m-m-morning."

Crawley's face was perfectly blank. The intelligent eyes behind the thick glasses looked straight at the news editor. "I don't remember. If you'll brief him, then."

When they were outside the news editor said, "If that doesn't beat anything for hard neck. It was y-your idea about the juvenile delinquency."

The features editor was shaking his head. Another three months and Crawley will have him out, he thought. Aloud he said, "It doesn't matter. We've got the story our way, haven't we? Let's go and talk to Frank."

Chapter Six

At almost the exact time on Friday morning that Edgar Crawley was calling his conference, Hugh Bennett was walking out of the reporters' room next door into *Editor Private*. There he found Mr Grayling, drinking a cup of tea. Mr Grayling was a small nervous man with a made-up bow tie that was never quite in place. He wore shirts that, even when they were in other respects perfectly clean, seemed always to have rather dirty cuffs, and he was equipped with upper and lower sets of false teeth that in moments of excitement clicked vigorously together.

"Sit down, Hugh. You were right at the heart of this sad business out at Far Wether last night, eh?"

Grayling had not seen the story on the previous night, but this seemed still a painfully obvious remark.

"It was a bit of luck," he said brightly. "Lane sent me out to do a story on the fireworks. It fell into my lap."

"Into your lap, yes. Precisely." Grayling was looking at the story, which he must surely have read before. "Excellent. A very well-written piece. My congratulations."

"Thank you."

Grayling sipped tea. His false teeth clattered. "Mr Corby was – ah – a friend of the chairman. He was a frequent visitor to the chairman's house."

"I see." And he did more or less see, with a certain sinking of the heart. The chairman, who owned a controlling interest in the paper, was a local building contractor named Weddle, an alderman and a prominent Methodist.

"I had a long conversation with the chairman this morning." Grayling polished the arm of his chair with his fist in a reflective manner. "He feels – and I found it difficult to disagree with what he said – that it is important to keep this unhappy affair in perspective. In relation, I mean, to other things happening in our city. We are a family paper, as you know. We have a tradition of sober and responsible journalism that has lasted more than half a century, Hugh. More than half a century."

"Do you mean my piece was irresponsible, sir, let the side down?"

Grayling's teeth chattered like a stick over railings. "By no means, Hugh. Haven't I said that it was excellent? It is just a question of the future treatment, that's all. We don't want to be sensational. Let us leave that for the nationals."

"You mean you don't want me to follow it up?"

Grayling moved his chair a half-turn so that it faced a picture of the chairman, his sharp teeth exposed in a rattish grin. "I would like you to follow it up, but with discretion. It is an unsavoury story. We shan't want too much about it."

"But this is a case of murder. It's not the kind of thing you can hush up."

"I am not suggesting any hushing up. We shall give an honest and full report of the story. It is a matter of local interest. But we shall treat it with discretion, Hugh, always with discretion."

He emerged full of useless anger. Clare was in the reporters' room, typing with two fingers. "You don't look as if the old man pinned a medal on your chest."

"He said it was a well-written piece, then made it clear he didn't want any more like it. Seems that the chairman was a friend of Corby's."

"Of *Mrs* Corby, you mean." A long narrow face, lined and seamed as the leather of a worn shoe, the narrow mouth set in a knowing grin, the whole topped with a great mass of curly grey hair, had appeared round the door. This was Roger Wills who, under the name of Farmer Roger, wrote the "Field and Farm" column that Corby had so much appreciated.

"Mrs Corby?" he said, astonished.

"Ah. That old cock our chairman has been on the soft nest a good many times, if you'll forgive the expression, my dear." Farmer Roger's dry old hand rested on Clare's buttocks, and she wriggled indignantly away. "There's none that's after their oats, if I may change the metaphor or would it be more like a simile now, more than your old Presbyterian Methodist Wesleyan kind of bible thumper. It's doing all that praying as gets their dander up. Though I'm a religious man myself," he said with an enormous wink.

"But Mrs Corby." It was difficult to connect that thin-nosed woman with feelings of desire, the act of love.

"A bit long in the tooth, I grant you that, but so's Weddle. Come on out, young Hugh, and I'll buy you a coffee."

As they walked down the High Street towards the Kardomah that was used by all the *Gazette* staff, Hugh Bennett marvelled at the number of people Farmer Roger knew, and at the facility with which he found a different descriptive phrase for each of them after they had gone by. Roger Wills had not, in fact, ever farmed for a living. He had an independent income and farmed as a hobby, experimenting with new types of seed, new kinds of mushroom spawn, vegetables that had never been grown in England. In his "Farm and Field" articles, however, which were often written in dialect and referred to fragments of local history, Farmer Roger treated farming with the seriousness that he had never given to it in life. In the office he was a licensed eccentric, and Hugh Bennett had a great admiration for him and for his column. Now as they sat opposite each other and drank their coffees Farmer Roger talked with his characteristic zestfulness, and Hugh wondered how much of what he said was true.

"My niece Angela lives just outside Far Wether, on the committee of the Women's Institute, hears all the gossip. She told me old Weddle was in there plenty of afternoons. Of course she's a Seventh Day Adventist Congregationalist sort of woman herself you know – Mrs C, I mean – and I dare say he was supposed to be calling on behalf of the Lord's Day Observance Society to stop smooching in haystacks on Sundays. But Weddle's an old ram, no doubt of that, got more girls in the family way than my prize bull."

"But Mrs Corby must be fifty." It seemed to him almost morally wrong that anybody over the age of thirty should experience sexual desire.

Farmer Roger's mouth opened in an O of laughter, the laugh revealing gums of palest pink, exquisite false small teeth. "Intolerant, that's what you are. It's all life, boy, don't you realise that, the great surging force that makes trees bud and walruses bark and dogs roll over. And the life force is good, that's what you young puritans don't understand who want to grab all the cakes and ale for yourselves. Take Braggart, my prize bull, now… "

When Farmer Roger was in the mood to comment on the affairs of life with this sort of racy wisdom, Hugh Bennett felt that he could listen for ever. And in fact they had another coffee, and he did listen for half an hour.

Chapter Seven

"Stabbed to death. And on Guy Fawkes night," the Chief Constable said. He shook his large fair head dismally. "Some wild party, I suppose, Langton."

"No, sir," Superintendent Langton said. "From our information there doesn't seem any doubt that it was a group of boys from the city. They came out on motorbikes and started throwing fireworks. Then they made this attack and went off. The whole thing didn't take more than a very few minutes."

"Anybody get the numbers of the bikes?"

"I haven't found anyone yet. They parked on the green and a good many of the residents were over at the fireworks."

"Any idea why they should – ah – have it in for this chap Kirby?"

"Corby, sir."

"Corby, then," the Chief Constable said, as though he were conceding a point. "Why should they stab him, can you tell me that?"

"Yes, I think so." Superintendent Langton was a square, dependable sort of man, rather slow of speech. He was not a favourite with the Chief Constable, who liked men to be visibly alert and spry, and found himself irritated by Langton's square dependableness. He had, in fact, little confidence in Langton, and now he tapped with a pencil on the desk and pulled at his long fair moustache while the superintendent was talking. "I was out at Far Wether last night, and talked to a good many of the locals. For that matter, I knew Corby well enough to pass the time of day. He was a self-important sort of a chap, liked to think of himself as the squire of the place, and it seems that a couple of weeks ago he threw out this same gang of roughs from a dance – "

"How d'you know they were the same? Anyone identify them?"

"Yes, sir," said Langton stolidly. "They shouted references about the dance. There was also a shouted reference to one of them named King, 'Get him, King,' something like that."

The Chief Constable swooped upon a glass of water on the desk, extracted a pill from his waistcoat, popped it into his mouth and swallowed. Langton tried not to let himself be disconcerted.

"Then it's likely that one at least of his assailants has blood on his clothing. Corby was stabbed four times in the chest by a thin-bladed knife, possibly by more than one knife, which has not yet been found."

Langton stopped. The Chief Constable waited to see if this was merely a longer pause than usual, but it seemed that the superintendent had finished. He walked over to the window and looked out at the damp mist as though he were pondering a course of action, although he had already made up his mind what to do. "You talk about a gang. I didn't know we had any gangs here."

"There are gangs of a sort in every big city, sir. I don't think ours are any worse than most. Or as bad."

"You've no idea who these boys might be?"

"No, sir. The stabbing took place only last night. I don't doubt that we shall have laid hands on them in the next couple of days."

"And what then?"

"What's that, sir?"

The Chief Constable spoke impatiently, as though repeating a lesson to a very dull pupil. "When you've found them, it's going to be very difficult to pin down this killer in a way to satisfy a jury. You say there may have been one knife or more than one, you talk about the assailant and then use the plural. It's not going to be easy to bring this home to an individual or individuals."

"Not easy, sir. But we shall do it."

"I think this is a case for Scotland Yard."

Langton was a slow man, but he was not insensitive. He knew that he irritated the Chief Constable, but he had not expected this. "But, sir – "

"Yes, Langton. Say your piece."

"This is a local crime. We know the people to look for, and how to find them. Anyone from London will have to learn from us." He formulated it slowly, hesitantly, conscious that he was not doing justice to his own case.

"Know the people to look for – that's just what you can't tell me. You've just said you've no idea who they are."

"The case isn't twenty-four hours old yet."

"Exactly. Now's the time to make up our minds. There's going to be a lot of fuss in the press about this, it's just the sort of case they enjoy. Give them a chance and they'll be right after us."

"Won't you give us a few days on it, sir?" Langton was conscious that he was losing the battle.

"I don't want you to think there's anything personal about this," the Chief Constable said, though they both knew that there was. "It's simply that it seems to me the sort of case which is bread and butter to Scotland Yard, whereas we're not really equipped to handle it. And if we're going to call them in, there's no use in hanging about. Quick's the word and sharp's the action, that's my motto." He stretched out his hand towards the telephone.

Chapter Eight

Within half an hour of the Chief Constable's telephone call to New Scotland Yard, Detective Superintendent Frederick Twicker had been assigned to the Guy Fawkes case. By lunch-time he had settled up or passed on the papers on his desk, had collected a change of clothing from his home in Hounslow, and was in the train with Detective Sergeant Norman. They ate lunch on the train, and over their bottles of beer Norman tried to induce Twicker to talk.

"They certainly got on the blower to us quickly enough. Surprising in a job of this sort. Generally the local boys like to keep it buttoned up tight."

Twicker chewed and masticated his roll, but did not reply.

"I reckon we're going to have to watch our steps a bit, tread a bit warily with the local boys."

"I always watch my step."

Twicker's tone was not encouraging, but Norman ignored that. "Yes, but you know what I mean. The local chap – what's his name, Langton – can be a lot of help or he can be a damned nuisance."

Twicker had been looking at the roast beef on his plate. Now he stared at the fleshily handsome sergeant, who stirred a little at the intensity of feeling in the dark eyes sunk deep in their sockets. "If he makes himself a nuisance, we shall have to deal with him."

Norman gave up, and after lunch settled down to his newspaper with occasional glances at Twicker, who for the most part stared out of the window.

Few people at the Yard cared very much about Twicker, and some were a little afraid of him. He had been involved in a case some years ago of which Norman had only a vague recollection, something about a confession that came unstuck. Norman was too young to know the details, but he had heard that Twicker's handling of this case had for a long time stopped him from getting promotion. He had never, in Norman's knowledge, been touched by the comradely feeling that pervades the CID, as it always pervades any organisation which is enclosed within another and yet retains its separate identity, as does the CID within Scotland Yard. Twicker would buy his round at the bar, but he was never – that was the simplest way to put it – he was never one of the boys. Yet, though he must be around fifty, he was still pretty much of a knockout to look at, with that mass of wavy iron-grey hair above sunken eyes, thin pointed nose and hard mouth. When's Twicker going to retire? Norman wondered as he settled back comfortably into his seat and looked at the superintendent's fine profile through half-closed eyes. What, he thought with a mental grin at his own cleverness, what makes Twicker tick?

Chapter Nine

Twicker did not care much for the Chief Constable. His manner was effusively friendly, and Twicker distrusted effusiveness. He had a large floppy fair moustache, which seemed to Twicker an affectation. And his manner towards Superintendent Langton had a shade of condescension which Twicker resented on Langton's behalf. He was accordingly well-disposed towards the stolid-looking local man.

"We've got a bit further since I rang this morning," the Chief Constable said, stroking his moustache. "There are three gangs in the city that Langton thinks may have been responsible, and Langton thinks he's narrowed it down further than that."

Langton took up the story. "'Gangs' is not quite the right word for these boys. There's not much night life here, but there are a few cafés where groups of boys hang out, playing records, drinking coffee, bringing in their girls after dances. Generally there's no harm in them, but in a group of a dozen boys you might find one or two who carried knives or did some petty pilfering or had been to an approved school. You know the sort of thing." Twicker nodded. "My idea is that one of these groups was responsible, that they went out to Far Wether meaning to rough Corby up a bit and it turned into something else."

" Murder," Twicker said without emphasis.

"Right. Now, one of these boys was called King – that is, more than one person on the scene heard a shout of 'Get him, King.' There's a lad named Jack Garney who runs around with a group of boys. They come from Peter Street and they're called the Peter Street lot, and they call Garney 'King.' We've picked up some of them this afternoon, and I'm proposing to ask them a few questions."

"I'll come with you." To the Chief Constable Twicker said, "That's what it is to know the ground and to know your local hoodlums. Superintendent Langton seems to have everything well under control."

Well, Norman thought, who'd have thought Twicker had it in him to pay a compliment? Langton's face showed nothing.

"Thought we'd go to the fountainhead," the Chief Constable said. "I don't doubt some of these young scoundrels did it, but proving it may be another matter."

"The boys all work in the same place, Page's Canning Factory," Langton said as they walked down the corridor afterwards. "And of course if they were in it together they'll have cooked up a story. This boy Garney is supposed to be pretty smart."

"They're never smart. They're hoodlums, that's all." Langton, who regarded his work impersonally, as a job like any other, was surprised by the bitterness in Twicker's voice.

They talked to the boys in small rooms with white-washed walls, furnished with hard chairs and chipped tables. Norman, with a police constable to take notes, took one boy, a local sergeant with another note-taker took another. Langton and Twicker talked to Garney.

And in spite of what Twicker had said, Garney was smart. Langton knew it after asking him no more than a couple of questions. Dark, thick, handsome, with hair brushed slickly upwards, he had a self-assured elegance which was genuine, as the seedy brightness of his Edwardian clothes was false.

He answered briskly. He had packed up work at half-past five last night, and had gone straight home. His mum had given him tea. He had hung about the house until a quarter to eight and had gone to a dance hall named the Rotor with his girl, Susie Haig. They had got to the Rotor just before eight o'clock and stayed there until ten-thirty. He had seen Susie home.

Corby had been killed between half-past six and a quarter to seven. Langton looked down at the papers in front of him.

"Do you know why I'm asking these questions?"

Garney said coolly, "Because of this bloke who got done last night out at Far Wether. You think I had something to do with it. Well, you're wrong."

"Did you go to a dance out at Far Wether a fortnight ago?"

"Yes."

"And there you had some trouble with Mr Corby."

Garney's broad shoulders shrugged in his tight green suit. "If that's who it was."

"He threw you out."

"We left. We don't go where we're not wanted."

"You're the leader of a gang called the Peter Street lot."

"It's not a gang. Just some of the boys.'

"But you're their leader."

"If they say so."

"I'm asking you." Garney shrugged again. "They call you King."

"Sort of a joke. Doesn't mean anything."

"One of them was heard to call out 'Get him, King,' last night."

The boy's self-assurance remained undisturbed. "Whoever heard that heard wrong."

"You still say you weren't out there last night?"

"I told you where I was, home till a quarter to eight." Garney smiled. "My mum will tell you the same. Then I took Susie to the Rotor. You talk to Susie."

"You think you've fixed up an alibi, don't you?"

"It's the truth."

"When your girl's been in here a few hours she'll talk." The palms of Langton's hands were flat on the table. "We know you were there last night, Garney. The sooner you admit it, the easier it's going to be for you."

"I went to the dance, I told you that already."

Twicker could have closed his eyes. He had heard a hundred, perhaps a thousand, interrogations like this, but carried out with infinitely greater skill, not in this bull-at-a-gate manner. Langton had his limitations, obviously. Twicker raised his grey eyebrows, and Langton nodded.

"Were your friends at this dance hall?" Twicker asked.

Garney looked at him, and hesitated for a moment.

"Yes."

"All of them?"

"Don't know what you mean by that."

"There are five of you in the Peter Street lot, aren't there?"

"Six," Garney said, and then looked as though he had bitten his tongue.

"Thank you for the information." Twicker smiled himself, not pleasantly. "And were they all at the Rotor?"

"I don't know. There was a pretty fair crowd."

"Which of them were there?"

"Ernie Bogan, Taffy Edwards, Les Gardner."

"Who are the others?

Langton was looking puzzled. "What's it matter who they were?" Garney burst out. "This bloke at Far Wether got done before seven, didn't he? What's it matter where we were at eight or nine?"

"Who are the others?" Twicker repeated.

"Rocky Jones. And Charkoff, we call him the Pole."

"They weren't at the Rotor?"

"I told you. It was crowded."

"Did you see them there?"

"I'm not saying. Ask them yourself. I'm not answering any more questions."

Twicker passed a note to Langton. It read: *Time for a change.* Langton said to the note-taker, "Look after him."

"What are you keeping me here for?" Garney said. "I want to go home."

"What was the point of those questions about the dance hall?" Langton asked when they were outside. "They rattled him all right, but why?"

"For one thing, Garney had primed the others on the rest of it, so they'll have their stories ready, but he hadn't bothered much about the dance hall because it was outside the time of the killing, so he's afraid they may get confused. But there's another thing. After something like this there are always one or two who lose their stomachs for it, get frightened, want to run away or confess. Those will be the ones who didn't go to the dance hall, stayed at home and cried their eyes out or told their mothers or got drunk. Jones and the Pole, they're the ones we put pressure on. They're the ones who're going to crack."

In a room farther down the corridor Norman was shouting at a thin, sallow boy of seventeen. The boy's English was not perfect, and sometimes he did not seem to understand the questions. This was the Pole, Charkoff. They listened to a few questions and then called Norman out of the room.

"What's his story?"

"Says he came home from work, had tea, went round to Ernie Bogan's house, watched television. Can't remember any of the programmes though he watched for an hour and a half. Then Ernie said he was going to a dance hall, but our boy felt sick, went home." Norman's broad mouth curled with distaste. "These bloody foreigners. Why don't they send 'em back where they came from?"

41

"That's a line." Norman looked surprised. Twicker said, "Take over Garney for a bit, will you. We've got nothing out of him. Make him tell his story all over again. We'll be back."

Norman walked away, and they went in to the Pole.

Twicker talked to him. His voice was quiet. "When did you come over from Poland?"

"Ten years ago. My mother and father, they escaped."

"You like it here?" There was alarm in Charkoff's eyes. "If you don't tell the truth we might send you to prison. Or back to Poland." Charkoff began to tremble. "The one who killed the man at Far Wether will go to prison."

"Not me. I didn't do it."

"You helped."

"No, no. I never helped. You must believe me. Please."

Now Charkoff was on his knees. Twicker felt no pity for his misery, as he had felt no admiration for Garney's self-assurance. "You were there. You took part."

"But I did nothing. Oh please, please."

"Then the best thing you can do is to make a statement, and tell us what did happen. Get up. Now, would you like to make a statement?"

"And then you will let me

Twicker's eyes met Langton's. "And then we shall let you go."

Charkoff dictated his statement, haltingly. Garney, he said, was the boss of the Peter Street lot, and it was he who had suggested going out to Far Wether and finding Corby. He said, "We will have fun with him," Charkoff said, turning his agonised eyes from one to the other of them. He had not taken a knife himself, but some of the others had taken knives.

"Just to have a bit of fun," said Langton, heavily ironical. Twicker frowned at him.

"Which of them took knives?"

"I don't know. I am not sure. Oh, please."

"Come on, now. Did Garney have a knife?"

"I think so, yes. King always carries a knife."

"But did you see him with it? You saw King with a knife, didn't you? He took it out and showed it to you?"

"No. I don't know. Oh, please do not ask me."

They spent half an hour on the knife question. In the end Charkoff thought that Garney, Edwards, Bogan and Gardner all had knives, but he was not sure. They had all thrown fireworks at Corby, he said, he had done so himself. But he had been away from the scrimmage that surrounded Corby, had not seen what happened, and had run for his motorbike only when somebody shouted, "Let's go." When they got back to the city Garney said they should all go along to the Rotor later on, and that if questions were asked they should provide alibis for each other during the earlier part of the evening. He had felt sick, and so he had not gone to the Rotor.

At the end of it, with the statement signed, Charkoff said, "That is all. Truly, that is all. May I go home now, please?"

"Maybe later."

"But you told me I could go home."

"When you tell us the truth, perhaps you will. You've got a bad memory about the knives."

"I have told you the truth. All I know I have told you."

"We'll let him cool off," Langton said. "I'll take one of the others."

Twicker nodded, left him, paid a visit to the local sergeant, Sterling, who had got nothing out of Gardner, and went back to Garney. He raised his eyebrows at Norman, who shook his head.

"All right, Garney," Twicker said. "Charkoff's told us the whole story. Here's what he said. The six of you went out to Far Wether. Four had knives, including you. You all threw fireworks, then you and Bogan fought with Corby. He saw you both stab him. Anything to say?"

43

"Yes. The Pole's a bloody liar. Or you are."

Twicker struck him sharply across the face. Garney gripped the seat of the chair.

"The super's funny," Norman said. "He doesn't like being called a bloody liar. Here, have a fag."

Garney accepted the cigarette distrustfully.

"The point is this," the sergeant went on. "You've got a case, too. You've got a story to tell. Before the super got this squeal from Charkoff I had another from Gardner. His story didn't fit with Charkoff's, not in every detail. You could put us straight on some of this, and it wouldn't do you any harm."

Garney puffed at the cigarette. "Go to hell."

"Did Bogan knife him? He was carrying a knife, that's right, isn't it? Was it Bogan who knifed him?"

"Let's go back to the beginning," Twicker said. "You went out to Far Wether that night intending to have a bit of fun with Corby."

Norman took it up. "Yes, can we agree on that? The six of you went out on your bikes to have a bit of fun."

"I've told you. I came home, had tea, hung about, went to the Rotor. I never went out to Far Wether."

They kept at it for another quarter of an hour without success. "That's it, then, I suppose," Twicker said.

He got up. Norman got up, stretched. Garney stood up too. They stared at him.

"Can I go now?"

"He may feel more talkative in the morning," Norman said.

"What's that stuff about the morning?" The boy, head lowered, looked from one to the other. "You going to charge me?"

Twicker stared at him from deep-set eyes. "Who said anything about charging you?"

"You can't keep me here all night without charging me. I know my rights."

"Listen to me." Twicker's voice was low, intense. "I don't like you, Garney. You're scum. For me, scum have got no rights. You understand?"

Garney began to shout. "I want my rights. I've been here for hours and nothing to eat. I want to go home."

Norman stared, astonished. "You want to go home. You really mean that?"

"You've got no right to keep me."

"I'll tell you what, Garney, did you notice the corridor outside?" Garney looked at Norman uneasily. "It's slippery, like a regular skating rink, you know what I mean? Somebody could slip on that and do himself an injury. I wouldn't like that to happen to you, Garney. And then it's treacherous weather. I said to the super as we came up the steps to the station, 'Those steps are dangerous,' I said. 'If somebody fell on them he might break a leg.' It wouldn't be safe for you to go home. You might hurt yourself." Norman sat down again. "Now, there are just a few questions we want you to answer, son, and then we might be able to find you a nice cup of tea. But mind, we want the right answers."

This also was routine, something that had been done and said ten thousand times in a hundred police stations, and Twicker, as he looked at Norman's fleshy face set in its mask of good humour, and at Garney's, in which fear was beginning to replace arrogance, felt nothing at all. Lies and tricks, threats and promises, these were the methods that brought results. Twicker did not doubt that they were much gentler than the methods used in almost every other country. Perhaps they were too gentle, for they got nothing out of Garney.

They got little out of the others, either, until they talked to Rocky Jones. Confronted by the admissions of Charkoff, Ernie Bogan, Taffy Edwards and Leslie Gardner all agreed that they had gone out to Far Wether, but all said that they had done nothing more than throw fireworks. All of them denied carrying knives. None of them had any idea who stabbed Corby.

It was nearly midnight when Sterling, the sergeant who had been questioning Rocky Jones, put his head round the door of the room in which Twicker was questioning Edwards. In the corridor Sterling said, "This one's ready to give."

"Has he said anything about the knives?"

"Not yet, sir. But he will. Would you like to take him?"

Jones was a small sand-coloured, weaselly figure. He shifted beneath the stare of Twicker's sunken eyes, and started like a jack-in-a-box at his first words. "How old are you?"

"Nineteen."

"Old enough to hang for murder."

"I didn't do anything." More rabbit now than weasel, Jones stared at Twicker.

"After what the others told us, that's what you'll get."

"Who – what did they tell you?"

Twicker looked at a sheet of paper. "Charkoff, Edwards, Gardner, they've all made statements."

"What did they say?"

"Enough." Twicker's mouth bit off the word. "We've got nothing to ask you."

"*Nothing* to ask me," Jones floundered, as though he had longed for nothing more than the chance of answering questions.

"Take him away."

"No, no. Please. I've got something to tell you."

"It's of no interest." Twicker was brusque.

"But it is. If they say I stabbed him it's not true. It was King."

Langton breathed a sigh. Twicker said, "All right. You can make a statement."

Jones's statement confirmed much of what Charkoff had said. He denied carrying a knife himself, but said that he had seen Garney's knife, and that Bogan and Gardner had been carrying them. Gardner was a particular friend of Garney's, and would do what Garney told him. When they left the city Garney had made imaginary cuts and slashes with his knife in the air, and had said, "This may come in handy." When the fireworks were thrown he had been close to Corby, together with Garney, Bogan and Gardner. Corby had been about to hit Bogan when Garney drew his knife. Somebody else had drawn a knife – he thought it was Gardner. Somebody – again he thought it was Gardner – had said, "Get him, King." Jones had seen a knife flash, and had heard Corby cry out. Then there had been a shout of "Let's go," and they had gone.

It took them three-quarters of an hour to get Jones's statement written down coherently. He was given a cup of tea and a sandwich and left quietly snivelling. Then Twicker, Langton, Norman and Sterling held a conference.

"What next?" Langton looked at Twicker. "We could certainly hold Garney now on what Jones says. One or two of the others as well, maybe."

"We want them all." Twicker's voice was deep in his throat.

"Let's hold them all as being concerned in the murder, sir," Norman said. "We've ample grounds for that. We can sort it out in the morning."

"And have the relatives learn they're under arrest, and destroy any evidence that's lying around? We want to get them in their homes. We'll do that tomorrow."

"Let them all go, you mean?" Langton said. "Garney too?"

"Garney too. We'll get them tomorrow, have a look round without a warrant."

"We want Garney inside. If he finds out that Jones has been singing I wouldn't like to be in Jones's shoes."

"If Jones has any sense he won't talk." Twicker's fingers were lacing and unlacing themselves. Norman saw with surprise that the superintendent was agitated. "And give them a little more rope. They'll use it the right way. Let them think they've fooled us."

"It's your decision," Langton said.

"That's right." Twicker stared at him.

They let the six boys go. It was one o'clock in the morning when Twicker and Norman returned to their hotel. "What a session," the sergeant said. "I'm out on my feet."

Twicker said nothing, but the last sound Norman heard before falling asleep was the scratch of pen on paper in the adjoining room. In the morning he was wakened by an insistent wasp-like buzz, and identified it as an electric razor operating in Twicker's bedroom. He looked at his watch. The time was six-fifteen.

Chapter Ten

On Friday Hugh Bennett did his follow-up stories for the nationals, stories which were designed to maintain interest in the murder and to earn some more linage. He was able to talk to his best police contact, PC Pickering, who had told him of the rumour that the CC was calling in Scotland Yard. On his last visit to the station he learned that some boys had been picked up for questioning, and also that the rumour about Scotland Yard had become a fact. There was too much routine work for him to get out to Far Wether as he would have liked to do, and he felt irritable and frustrated as he opened the door of the Pile Street flat, and walked up past the smell of cabbages. There were voices in the living-room.

Michael was sitting on the sofa with broken springs, and a girl sat deep in the room's one comfortable chair. "Hugh, this is Jill Gardner," Michael said. "We've been waiting for you. What's the news on Guy Fawkes?"

This was the poppet. She did not get out of the chair, and he had no more than an impression, at this first glance, of blue eyes set wide apart, a snub nose, slim legs.

"We're drinking beer," Michael said. "The poor man's substitute for a genuine intoxicant. Jill's brother seems to be mixed up in this Guy Fawkes business.

"Your brother?" He paused with the glass at his mouth.

"They've taken him in for questioning. Have you heard about it?" Michael's tone seemed deliberately light. The girl, after that first look at him, stared at the worn Indian carpet.

"They've got half a dozen boys in. I don't know their names."

"My brother Leslie is one of them. He goes about with a boy named Jack Garney and some others. They call themselves the Peter Street lot." There was a breathlessness about her voice that he found attractive.

"Is one of them named King?"

"They call Jack Garney 'King.' "

"He's their leader?"

"I suppose so. They're like children, playing games. What's going to happen to Leslie, Mr Bennett?"

"They'll ask him questions. Was he there, did he see anything, that sort of thing."

"A sort of third degree."

He said with a confidence he did not feel, "There's no third degree here. But one of the boys was called King, I heard another one use the name. So your brother may have been there." There was a question in his voice, which she ignored. "Has your brother been in trouble with the police?"

"He and another boy called Bogan took a car for a joyride eighteen months ago. They were bound over. We live in Peter Street and it's fairly rough down there. I don't suppose you know it."

"You can call him Hugh," Michael said.

"But Leslie would never have anything to do with violence. He's rather timid really."

"Does he carry a knife?"

"I told you. He's not a violent boy."

"I'm sorry. It's the sort of question the police will ask if they believe he was there."

"I suppose so. Ever since mother died five years ago I've tried to keep Leslie away from – I don't know what I can call it but bad influences. They don't like me much in Peter Street. I'm a schoolteacher, and that isn't approved of, and they don't like me trying to look after Leslie either." She smiled briefly, and he was aware of a core of resolution. Inside the poppet was a character.

"Was your brother at Far Wether last night?"

She stared at him. "I don't know. But if he was, I know Leslie well enough to be sure that he had nothing to do with that man's death."

The bell rang. Michael, muttering something, ran down the stairs. The girl stood up, and looked at him almost with hostility. "If Leslie is in trouble I'm going to get him out of it. I should like any help I can get."

There were feet on the stairs, voices. Michael came in, looking slightly self-conscious. "This really is the press, the man from the city, big-time stuff. Frank Fairfield from the *Banner.*"

Behind Michael there entered a great wreck of a man, a handsome ruin. The handsomeness was a thing of the past now, the nose was drink-reddened and threaded with lines, there were thin red threads in the bewildered eyes behind horn-rimmed spectacles. Shabby clothes flapped on a great frame, there was a button off the raincoat, the thick brown shoes needed heeling. The man blinked and peered a little, and spoke with an agreeable hesitancy.

"Please, look, don't let me break anything up. They sent me round here from your office. An awful nerve, to come busting in. You're Hugh Bennett."

"And this is Jill Gardner. Her brother's been taken for questioning." Michael said to the girl, with no trace of his usual languor – rather, indeed, like a salesman pushing a new line of goods, "Frank Fairfield, Fleet Street's ace crime reporter. Have some beer."

The hand that took the beer trembled, the large spatulate fingers were slightly dirty. "I'm down here on some whim of my lord and master's," Fairfield said apologetically. "And when he speaks it isn't mine to question why. It doesn't honestly seem much of a story. What do you think now?"

There was something agreeable about the putting of such a question, as though he were an authority on whether it was a good story or not, and it was a question that seemed to be asked guilelessly, without the least intention of flattery. Fairfield nodded while Hugh talked about the case, and seemed to be listening with every appearance of attention, when suddenly he said, "Shall we adjourn to the local and have a drink with the *Banner?*"

"A drink with the *Banner,* splendid idea," Michael said.

Jill Gardner said, "I think I ought to try to find out what's happened to Leslie. They called for him at the factory, just after he signed off."

"A quarter to nine. He won't be back yet." Fairfield spoke with complete assurance. "And I'd like very much to talk to you, Miss Gardner. It may sound ridiculous, but perhaps the *Banner* might be able to help."

They were in the Crown and Anchor, round the corner, by the time he amplified this remark. He spoke almost apologetically. "People think newspapers do a great deal of harm, intrusion into private lives and all that. Perfectly true, of course. But they can do some good. That's true, too. If I didn't think so I wouldn't be here. And I've been a newspaperman five times as long as you two boys put together." He lapsed into silence, swilling the beer round his glass.

"How can you help my brother?"

Fairfield looked up at her. He was not in the least drunk, yet there was something blurred about him, as though he saw hazily some kind of vision that for the rest of them simply wasn't there. "Publicity." There was again a silence before he amplified this. "Let your brother tell his story. Let the other boys do the same. We'll print them."

"I don't know"

"My dear Miss Gardner, what in the world have you got to lose? It can't hurt him to talk. Does he work tomorrow?"

"Tomorrow. Oh, it's Saturday. No, he doesn't."

"May I come round at ten o'clock, then?"

"I suppose so. I'm sorry about the way I sound, suspicious you might call it. My father doesn't like newspapers. The truth is, I'm rather muddled."

"It's a muddled world." It seemed that Fairfield was about to make some further, vital pronouncement, but instead he transferred his gaze to the two young men. "Why are you in the provinces?"

"Because we're ugly ducklings who are turning into geese." This synthetic persistent brightness of Michael's jarred on Hugh. He said, knowing that he sounded quarrelsome or silly, "What's wrong with being a provincial journalist?"

"A contradiction in terms. In the provinces you work on a paper. You are hardly a journalist."

"I think I ought to go," Jill Gardner said.

Fairfield raised his slightly shaking hand. "Let Hugh telephone the station first. From what I remember of life in the provinces Hugh will have a contact in the police – "

"So have I." That was Michael.

"And so have you. Of course. If Hugh telephones his contact we may find out what's happening to Leslie."

Hugh made the call from a box on the first floor. PC Pickering was surprised that he knew Gardner's name, wouldn't say anything about the other boys under questioning.

"Oh, come on, Bob, I know the Peter Street lot."

On the telephone Bob Pickering's voice had almost lost its local burr. "This is a murder case."

"You won't give me any names?"

"I can't tell you anything more."

"At least you can say this. Has Gardner been released yet, or is he being held?"

"Nobody brought in for questioning has yet been released."

"When do you suppose – ?"

He was cut off. Evidently Pickering was not alone. When he told them what had been said, Jill Gardner got up. Michael was talking to Fairfield, and seemed hardly to notice that she was going. But Fairfield noticed. "Good night, Miss Gardner. Ten o'clock in the morning."

Hugh went with her to the door. "Where are you going?"

"It doesn't look as though I shall get anything from the station. I must go home and tell father. He'll be upset."

"Of course."

"Yes, but you don't realise – well, it doesn't matter. You've been kind."

"I've done nothing. Look, I may come along with Fairfield in the morning. If I can manage to get away from the office, and it's all right with you."

"Glad to see you." Before he could be sure that those were her actual words, she added, "There's my tram," waved and was gone.

He went back. Michael, bright-eyed, was telling stories that he had heard before – malicious, slightly witty little stories about the office and what went on in it, stories designed to show the faint absurdity of Clare and Farmer Roger and Grayling and the rest. Hugh was faintly shocked, feeling that this was in some way a betrayal of the people they worked with. And if he were not there, what would Michael be saying about him? Fairfield listened, drinking pint upon pint of beer, the glance of his glazed eyes shifting occasionally from Michael to Hugh, and back again. He said little, speaking with emphasis only when Michael suggested telephoning the station again.

"No. Don't push it. Your pal won't like you pressing him too hard, makes him look a bit silly. Leave it for the night."

"Okay, big shot," Michael said. He started another story. Fairfield, or the *Banner,* paid for another round of drinks. They stayed until the pub closed. On the way back to the flat Hugh said, "You left her pretty much in the lurch."

"What, our Miss Gardner? She knows the way home, I suppose. If not, she shouldn't be out. Besides, I thought you were interested."

"I liked her."

"She's all yours, boy. Too prissy for me. Old Fairfield's a bit of a dead-beat, isn't he?"

Hugh did not reply.

Chapter Eleven

There was nothing particularly sordid about Peter Street, yet it was undoubtedly a depressing place. Peter Street, Melantha Street, Philidor Street, Bute Street, Anderson Street – these names chosen at apparent random designated streets that seemed identical in their two up and two down respectableness. Most of the children were clean where twenty years ago they would have been dirty, they wore shoes where they would have gone barefoot, but they still played hopscotch on the pavement and scrawled goal-posts on a wall. Fairfield talked philosophically about these things to Hugh as they got off the tram and made their way through Melantha and Philidor and Bute Streets on a grey wet Saturday morning.

"The trouble with the welfare state is it's done too much, and yet it hasn't done enough. It gives these working chaps money, but what are they going to do with it after they've bought a telly and a fridge? Look at them." He pointed to some long-haired boys wearing drainpipe trousers and tight-fitting overcoats, who talked and giggled by a lamp-post. "All dressed up, money in their pockets, nowhere to go. That's how gangs begin. You get a boy like this kid Garney, who's a natural leader from all accounts. He has to show the others how smart he is. He's the kind of boy that we make an officer in wartime, probably he volunteers for a commando unit, kills a few people, comes home a hero. When there isn't a war on we've got no use for him. It's bloody ironical."

"I thought the *Banner* was a Tory paper."

Fairfield laughed, deep and rich. "So it is, Hugh boy, so it is. And so am I. This isn't party politics, just common sense. A great guide to life, common sense. Do you know why we came down here by tram instead of taxi? Because we may want to talk to some of these people. Coming in a taxi, paying off the driver, giving a tip, is liable to put them off. Ever heard of Twicker?"

"The Scotland Yard man who's come down? No, I haven't."

"He's an odd character. I could a tale unfold about Twicker, and perhaps I will some day. Here we are."

The iron gate creaked a little. Fairfield lifted the knocker. At the upper window of the house next door the corner of a lace curtain was raised and lowered. The door of the house opened and a big man, thick-browed, with shirt-sleeves rolled up to show hairy arms, stood in the doorway.

"I know you," he said to Hugh. "Bennett your name is. Remember me? George Gardner, secretary Paradise Vale ward of the Labour Party. You've been to a couple of our meetings."

Hugh remembered. Gardner was a leading member of a Left Wing ginger group inside the Labour Party. He was also on the local council. "And you're Fairfield. My daughter told me about you. Come in." He shouted: "Jill."

He led them into a front room neatly tidy, conscientiously bright, with its unused-looking three-piece suite, and reproductions of Van Gogh and Utrillo on the walls. Jill Gardner came in and sat down without saying anything. Gardner stood with his back to the tiled fireplace.

"Les is still asleep. They picked him up after work, didn't let him go until after midnight. That's what they call interrogation." He looked directly at Fairfield. "Now, I don't know what Jill said last night but whatever it was, I'm telling you now that we've got nothing to say to the press. Any of us. Am I making myself clear?"

"You're speaking clearly enough," Fairfield said. "But you don't make sense."

"I know what you want." A thick finger pointed at Fairfield, jabbed as it had done at a hundred meetings. "Supposing one of us tells you there's a few rough lads in Peter Street, you twist it round and talk about gang warfare. Nothing of the sort. There's nothing wrong with Peter Street that the people who live in it can't cure. I've brought up two children in it and there's nothing wrong with them. They're decent and honest. Will you say that? Not you. It's your job to live by peddling lies."

"Dad," Jill said. Her protest, Hugh felt, was automatic.

"Nothing personal," Gardner said, unperturbed.

Fairfield's fingers, as he took out a cigarette, were as shaky as they had been the night before. His voice had no trace of anger. It was the same hesitant, cultured yet classless voice that Hugh Bennett had heard the night before, and the fact that he might have been debating some point on a television brains trust gave his words an extra sting.

"You know, you're the sort that makes press reporters and photographers and everyone else behave badly. You've stayed in Peter Street, I'd like to take a bet on it, because you're a Labour man and proud of it. You don't want to move to a neighbourhood one step up, where the houses have bits of gardens front and back – "

"I'm Labour and proud of it, yes. I stay with my own sort. And there's nothing wrong with this house. We've put in a bathroom."

"That makes it perfect," Fairfield said. "What about your family? Ever think of them?"

"We've been happy here." Jill's cheeks were red. "You don't have to listen to him, Dad."

The thick brows were turned on her. "I let every man have his say."

"If they were happy it was because you told them to be. Told them what a splendid thing it is to live in a slum and help to make it a better place. But was your son all that happy?"

"Leslie is a good boy."

"He seems to have been running round with some bad ones. Then I come round. You know my name, you don't like the *Banner* – "

"I think it stinks." The big man thrust his head forward as he said it.

"Right. Now, my job is to find out the truth about this case. Not lies, the truth, you understand? That's the way journalism works, it's what reporters are there for. You won't let me get at the facts through you. Then I'll have to do it through someone else." Fairfield put down his cigarette. "You won't let me talk to your son, probably won't even let me have a picture of him. Then we have to do these things another way. Don't blame me for it."

Now Gardner's voice rose in savage irony. It was the sort of voice Bennett had heard him use to crush opposition argument at the Paradise Vale branch meetings. "You mean, don't blame you because when people won't let you through the front entrance you have to wriggle through a window at the back. Well, if I catch you wriggling in the back way here you'll be sorry. I'll tell you this. My son had nothing to do with what happened at Far Wether on Guy Fawkes night, and that's all I'm saying. And you'll get no more out of anybody else in this household."

Fairfield got up and Hugh Bennett, feeling like an actor without a speaking part, got up too. Jill said, to him rather than to Fairfield, "I'm sorry." She opened the front door.

59

Two policemen were standing outside it, a black maria was just down the road, and it seemed that half the population of Peter Street was crowded round it.

The policeman in front was a sergeant. " 'Morning," he said.

Gardner stood with hands on hips, blocking the entrance. " 'Morning to you, Joe Malcolm. What do you want?"

"I should like to speak to Leslie Gardner."

"He's asleep."

"Then you'd better wake him up." With a backward jerk of the head, the sergeant said, "It might be easier if we came in."

Gardner did not move. The sergeant shrugged.

"Have it your own way. Tell him to come down. At once."

"Why should I?"

The sergeant showed a piece of paper in his hand. Gardner looked at it, then shouted, "Les."

A slim, pale boy, wearing shirt and trousers, came down. He was strikingly like his sister.

"Leslie Gardner," the sergeant said, "I have here a warrant for your arrest as being concerned in the murder of one James Renton Corby, on the green at Far Wether, on the night of November the fifth. I have to warn you – "

The boy stared at the sergeant and then at his father, who looked back at him with a face of stone. Then it was as though the boy suddenly, and for the space of a few seconds, took wings. He must, in fact, have jumped, but the effect was that of his rising suddenly into the air over the sergeant's outstretched hands, landing miraculously past them, diving round and away from the other policeman, and so out into the street. Then he began to run, tripped over a projecting kerbstone and fell. The two policemen caught and lifted him, not gently. They had practically to carry him to the black maria. He passed close to Hugh, who saw the trembling mouth that was whispering "Dad" and "Jill" and "Please," the trickle of blood at the forehead, the staring eyes. He had a glimpse of other faces inside the black maria, of words incoherently shouted, fists raised. Then the van drove off, people crowded round, the street bubbled with conversation.

"Bastards, those rotten bastards, sneaking up, taking away the kids."

"Just kids, that's all."

"Thing is, you know what caused it, King and some of the others went round to see Rocky and the Pole, told them to keep their mouths shut. Rocky got the wind up, did a bunk."

A thin-nosed, sandy, ferrety man spoke to Gardner, not without malice. "Looks as if we're in the same boat, eh, George? Going to use your influence with the council to get your boy out?"

Somehow Frank Fairfield was beside the man, saying something to him. "I'm Mr Jones from No.32. They had my boy in last night, kept him for hours. Then when they did let him out the others threatened him, told him they'd cut him up..."

Fairfield had him by the arm now, they moved away down the street. Gardner looked at them all, then turned abruptly and went back into the house. Jill followed her father and shut the door. Hugh walked down Peter Street, and away from it. He had suffered the kind of shock that comes only to those romantics who do not link their own experiences with life as it goes on around them. There was really no reason at all why he should have been shocked by his recognition of Leslie Gardner as the youth who had pushed over the little girl on Guy Fawkes night.

Chapter Twelve

Twicker and Norman were met by the news as soon as they got to the station that morning. Langton said without apparent emotion, "One of those boys has done a bunk."

It was not for Norman to comment, but he would have liked Twicker better if the superintendent hadn't preserved such a sphingine immobility, hadn't said merely, "Which one?"

"Jones. The boy who sang last night. His father, nasty piece of work in a small way, been inside a couple of times for petty pilfering, rang this morning early. He said after his boy came home last night a note was pushed through the letter-box. Jones didn't see the note himself, and can't find it now, but he says when the boy opened it he was frightened, said the others were going to cut him up. The way he talked, young Jones might have been a shy violet instead of a little rat who's had his nose in the gutter ever since he left the cradle. So it seems he got the wind up and skipped. Not likely he'll get far," Langton added, but there was no comfort in his tone.

There was something inhuman, Norman felt, about Twicker's calmness. To have his decision of the previous night so clearly shown as mistaken, to have to make a report which couldn't possibly be a justification, to have to inform the Chief Constable, these were painful humiliations. It would have got Langton on his side if the super had admitted that he'd guessed wrong last night, or if that was too much to ask, had at least let go a few comradely curses. But Twicker simply made a gesture in the direction of the Chief Constable's room and said, "He knows about it?"

Langton nodded. "That's done."

"Good. Then we'd better bring in the other five." Twicker turned to Norman. "I'll have a word with the CC now, then we'll go out to Far Wether. If you can come with us I'd be pleased," he said to Langton.

It was an olive branch extended reluctantly and too late. Langton said stiffly, "I've got a lot on around here this morning. The local chap – his name's Buckley – can help you with the people out there more than I can."

Twicker merely nodded. It was an object lesson, Norman thought, in how to lose friends and alienate people. As they left the station it began to rain.

Late that afternoon Norman typed up the notes of what they had got from people at Far Wether. He had got very wet, and was not in a good temper. Not for the first time, he thought that a detective's life had little to recommend it. This was Saturday afternoon, and he might have been at home with his feet up in front of a roaring fire eating buttered toast, after an afternoon spent watching Fulham at Craven Cottage. Instead, he was sitting in a cold and draughty room typing out a mass of boring notes in a case that was likely to provide glory for nobody, and certainly none for Sergeant Norman, after eating a stale bun and drinking a cup of tea. It was a hard life, he thought, deliberately putting out of mind how much he enjoyed the drinking and the comradeship and the feeling that he belonged to an élite which possessed powers denied to the rest of society. And there's not a piece of crumpet in the case, he thought, I dare say there's not a piece of crumpet in this whole dead-and-alive city. He twisted the paper round the platen and began to type.

Joe Pickett. Age 45. Works as jobbing gardener at various houses in district. Attended dance, saw Corby throw out boys. Said that actually at dance Corby was involved in struggle with only two boys, others left. Confident he would recognise these two again, and probably others. Close to Corby on Guy Fawkes night. Saw him attacked. Saw two boys actually strike blows. Saw a knife drawn by one boy, not sure which one. Heard a voice cry, "Get him, King." Called out to boys to stop. Saw boys run away.

Joshua Mackintosh. Age 52. Local doctor. Not at dance, but present on Guy Fawkes night. Confirms Pickett's story, except that he says "two or three" boys attacked Corby. Thinks he might recognise one of them. Examined Corby immediately after attack, and will give evidence as to injuries.

Maureen Dyer. Age 11. Daughter of local farmer. Present on Guy Fawkes night. One youth stumbled against her, knocked her over. She felt in his pocket "something hard and sharp." Saw youth clearly, thinks she would recognise him again.

There was a lot more of it, but the rest was unimportant. These were the witnesses who had really seen something of the boys and who might be able to identify them. There was the reporter from the *Gazette*, too, but Twicker, a glutton for work, was looking after that himself.

Chapter Thirteen

Clare Lurched on her high heels across the Reporters' Room and said with haughty archness, "Your sins have found you out."

"What?" It was half-past five, and the office was deserted. Hugh Bennett, there only because he was duty reporter for the evening, was dozing over *Of Human Bondage*.

"Don't look so alarmed, sweetie. It's a police superintendent, a real one all the way from Scotland Yard. I met him on the doorstep and brought him in."

He blinked back sleep and said to the man who stood a little behind and to one side of Clare, "Oh yes. I'm sorry. You're – "

"My name is Twicker." The voice was low and impersonal. "I wanted to have a word with you, Mr Bennett. I shan't keep you long."

"Of course."

"Thank you for your help," Twicker said to Clare, speaking rather as though she were a child. Clare, who had, as Hugh knew, a belief that she was attractive to what she called older men, looked annoyed. He did his best for her.

"This is Clare Cavendish, one of our reporters."

"Sometime," Clare said with ghastly vivacity, as Twicker gravely bowed his grey head in acknowledgement of her name, "sometime I'd like to interview you, Superintendent, so that I could do a piece for my women's page. Something absolutely personal, you know. What you eat for breakfast, whether you take the dog for a walk at night, funny things that have happened to you – you know?"

"You're confusing me with a celebrity, Miss Cavendish." Twicker turned away from her so decisively that Clare had no choice but to leave. She made a face at Hugh just before closing the door.

Hugh shivered. He felt cold, in spite of the electric radiator's shining bars, and was still not fully awake.

"It's about the Far Wether business, I suppose."

"Yes. My sergeant and I were out there today. We took a number of statements. You were there yourself." There was something uncomfortably intense in Twicker's gaze. What was it Fairfield had said about him? "What I want you to do is to tell me just what you heard and saw that evening."

"You mean I shall be called as a witness."

The superintendent smiled briefly. "We haven't got as far as calling witnesses yet. We take dozens of statements, hundreds perhaps, in a matter like this. You know that, I'm sure. This is just routine."

Had all this happened less than two days ago? Hugh wondered as he told haltingly of that evening, trying to remember and trying also, what seemed somehow even harder, not to invent, not to clarify artificially something that was in essence confused. Twicker made a note or two, but for the most part sat and listened. At the end he said, "This youth – you had your arms round him – did you recognise him? And would you know him again?"

It was quiet in the room that was often so noisy, and Hugh Bennett took in the room's details, the pipes resting on an inkstand at Lane's desk, the open typewriters, the copies of *Vogue* and *Harper's* stacked neatly at Clare's place, the general genial familiarity of chipped old desks and yellowing curled notices pinned up on the walls. One of the juniors had left a piece of paper in the very old Oliver that was reserved for junior staff and, straining his eyes to look, he saw that it said in capitals GOD IS LOVE BUT LANE IS OUR NEWS EDITOR.

"Did you recognise him?" Twicker repeated without impatience.

Why should he notice these things at this moment, why should what he said seem important? "Yes," he said, and began immediate qualification. "That is, I didn't recognise him at the time, but I've seen him since and recognised him."

"When?"

"This morning. I was in Peter Street when he was arrested. His name is Leslie Gardner."

Twicker's deep-set eyes stared uncomfortably at him. "You are sure this was the same boy?"

His boats were burnt now, and rightly burnt. "Quite sure."

"When he left you, he went towards Corby?"

"Yes."

"This was before you heard somebody shout, 'Get him, King'?"

"Yes."

"Do you think you would recognise the voice of the boy who said that?"

He tried to evoke the voice, to catch any flavour of individuality in it, and failed. "I don't know."

"That's all, then." Then Twicker said with apparent casualness, "When you had your arms round Gardner, did you feel anything in his pockets?"

"In his pockets." He considered, trying to stretch out those few seconds of contact. "Yes. I came up against something hard on his right-hand side. I wouldn't like to say which pocket."

"Could you feel what sort of shape it was? Could it have been a knife?"

"It could have been, yes."

"All right." Twicker got up. "I'd like you to come down to the station and make a statement, when it's convenient. Tomorrow morning?"

"Yes." A shade too eagerly perhaps, he said, "Is there anything you can tell me for the *Gazette*?"

"We have made five arrests in connection with the murder." Twicker spoke slowly. He was a remarkably handsome man, Hugh thought. "We believe that a sixth boy, Frank Jones, can help us with our inquiries. We are anxious to interview him."

"You can't say more than that?"

"Not at the moment. A man has been killed, and I'm here to find out who did it. To you this may be just a piece of copy, but to me it's something personal."

Was it true, Hugh wondered after Twicker had gone, that to him the case was just a piece of copy? He read again what that over-bright junior had written: GOD IS LOVE BUT LANE IS OUR NEWS EDITOR. Then, for no particular reason, he began to think about Jill Gardner.

Chapter Fourteen

The Rotor was in Yates Road, the main street of Paradise Vale. It stood, blinking its name in neon, between a multiple clothing store and a multiple grocer, both of which were closed on this Saturday evening. Norman pushed open the swing-door and went in. He was feeling much more cheerful since Twicker had given him the job of making inquiries here, even though the accompanying remark that this was the kind of thing Norman did well might not be taken as wholly complimentary. Now his fleshy nose sniffed something, as he would have put it, that you could get your teeth into, in this world with its dance music heard beyond a farther door, its voices and laughter and its rich feminine smell. He looked deliberately at the pay-desk girl, a spotty brunette who wore a sky-blue pill-box hat, a darker blue jersey and yellow tights, and said, "I want to see the manager."

"Mr Nicholas? But you haven't paid."

Norman showed his fine big teeth in a smile. "I didn't say I wanted to go in. Just to see the manager."

"Is it a complaint?"

"I'll tell him when I see him, shall I?" Norman's smile broadened. He showed her his badge.

"A real detective."

"I'm really real. Would you like to pinch me to make sure?" He offered her a thick arm.

"I'll tell Mr Nicholas." She called another girl to the pay-desk, whispered something, and disappeared. Norman felt pleasure in the pit of his stomach. The moments that generated this feeling of warm pleasure provided the reason, or one reason, for being a detective. When the girl had come back and taken him to Mr Nicholas the sensation did not diminish. Small, alert, uncertain, and very hairy – bushes of hair sprang from his ears and cheek-bones, and covered the backs of his hands – Mr Nicholas represented a type that Norman instantly recognised as his natural victim. He accepted the whisky that was poured for him, refused a cigarette, and put his thick body into a comfortable chair.

"You're a stranger here, Mr – "

"Norman. Detective Sergeant Norman. That's right."

Mr Nicholas shot his cuffs over his hairy hands, and said with a mixture of boldness and uncertainty, "And what brings you to the Rotor? What have we been doing wrong?"

"Have you been doing something wrong?" He felt the whisky go down.

"I hope not, Sergeant."

"I hope not, too." They both laughed. "But you've been keeping some rather bad company."

"This is a respectable dance hall. We have had no trouble for more than a year – "

With discourteous heaviness Norman interrupted. "Some boys who call themselves the Peter Street lot come in here."

The little man spread out his hands. "I am afraid – I do not think I know them."

"You ought to. They're bossed by a kid named Garney. They call him King."

"Ah, Garney." Mr Nicholas rubbed his hands with pleasure at the identification. "I know him. And some of his friends."

"They're bad company." Norman swilled round the rest of the whisky, sloshed it down. "They've been arrested for murder. You hadn't heard? And the thing that interests us is that they were in here on Thursday night shortly after the job was done, fixing a bit of an alibi. Looks as though they found the Rotor a convenient place."

"But – " Mr Nicholas tried hard to be outraged.

"Maybe you had nothing to do with it. But we want your help. You help us, we'll help you," Norman said meaninglessly.

There was silence. The little man looked at Norman's glass, poured more whisky.

"It's the job out at Far Wether, I expect you've heard about it?"

"No. Mostly I read a Greek paper."

"You're living in England now, you want to read an English paper." Mr Nicholas smiled, trying to pretend that this was a joke. "There was a man stabbed to death on Guy Fawkes night, and we think Garney and his friends did it. Later on they came in here, or some of 'em did. Now, I want to talk to anyone who talked to them that night, you understand. I want to know what they did and what they said."

"I understand. You should talk first to my chief hostess, her name is Jean Willard. She is a pretty girl."

"Good," Norman said heartily. "I like to talk to a pretty girl. Then I shall want a place to talk to her."

"Yes. You will please use this office."

"Thanks. You've been very co-operative. I appreciate that."

"And now I will go downstairs and send Jean up to you."

"I'll just come with you," Norman said. "It's not that I don't trust you, an Englishman always trusts a Greek until he finds out better, but I'd just like to break the news to Jean myself."

It was a dance hall like half a dozen in London suburbs, and Norman saw that Nicholas had not been lying when he said it was respectable. Or upon the whole respectable. Sixty per cent of the people there were office workers, typists, secretaries, bookkeepers, and their young men. There was another ten per cent, it might be, of older men who were dancing with the hostesses and looking out for girls. The rest were a job lot, boys with thick sideboards and brightly coloured suits, slick but untidy girls in jeans, their social differences blended by an identity of dress. Half a dozen girls sat together talking, and Mr Nicholas tapped one of them on the shoulder.

The girl turned round. Her mouth was a pencil line, artificially shaped into a bow, and she was chewing gum. She looked at Norman and said, with an assumed American accent, "You want to dance?"

"No. My name's Norman, CID, Scotland Yard. I believe you may be able to help me."

"You do?" She did not stop chewing.

"Anything that you can do to help this gentleman you will please do, Jean," Mr Nicholas said earnestly.

"Can I buy you a drink?" But the Rotor had no licence. He nodded to Nicholas, who scuttled away among the dancers, bought two Coca Colas and sat down with the girl at a metal table. She sucked up the drink through a straw. "It's about King on Thursday night, that right?"

"And the others. You know King well?"

"I ought to. I used to be his girl."

" Used to be?"

"He's been going with Susie Haig the last few weeks. She's not here tonight."

"Who broke it up?"

"None of your business." Somehow the girl managed to chew and to drink at the same time. "It was mutual."

"Perhaps you didn't like the boys he was going round with?"

"Look, mister, you'd better ask me straight out what it is you want to know. If I feel like answering I will, and if not I'll say so."

Norman had not tasted his Coca Cola, and now he pushed it aside. He felt anger rising within him. He put a hand on her thin arm. Her voice rose.

"Take your hand off me."

"Listen," Norman said furiously. "You can come with me up to your boss's room or you can come down to the station, I don't care which. Make up your mind."

The cupid's bow curved in a smile. "All right, let's go upstairs. But leave go of my arm, you're hurting."

He followed her upstairs. She had a good figure with stringy, but well-shaped legs. In Nicholas' office he sat on the desk. The whisky bottle had been left out, and he poured them both whisky. Away from the music and the bodies moving in their unbroken clinch round the dance floor he felt more relaxed.

"First things first. Your name's Jean Willard, and you've been here – how long?"

"Eighteen months."

"So you know what's going on. Now, Jean, Garney and some of his pals came in on Thursday night." He paused, but she did not answer. "I want to know how they looked, who they talked to, what they said."

"You don't want much." A little whisky slopped over on her chin. She wiped it away and leaned forward, her body straining at the purplish frock she wore. "By what you say, these boys cut up the chap out at Far Wether. What's to stop them doing me?"

"We'll stop them," Norman said without confidence. "We'll give you a guard."

She sneered. "Thank you for nothing. What happens when you take him away? I tell you, I should have to leave this place."

"Why not?"

She stared at him in surprise, her mouth slightly open. "Why not?"

"You belong in London." Norman felt a warmth in his stomach as he said it. How old are you now, Miss Willard? he silently asked. Twenty-one? Let Gipsy Norman tell your future in the crystal ball. I see you going to London, strip-teasing in a club, finding yourself a ponce and working hard for him, ending as a madam if you're lucky, and it's an end that won't be so very far from your beginning in point of time. Oh yes, you belong in London, Miss Willard. "What is there for you down here? What sort of place is this? What money do you make? I don't see why you want to stay."

"There was King."

"Tell me about him."

"We'd been going together for six months. He's nice. Well, you know, exciting. All the boys looked up to him, it really was something to go around with him."

"He looks a big boy here, he'd be a tadpole where the big fish swim."

She had stopped chewing. Now she began again. "You don't talk much like a copper."

"We're like anybody else only more so. We know the score. I could help you get out of here." Norman's exophthalmic eyes met her withdrawn, dark, beady look. I bet she's a wonderful lay, he thought. "You can look after yourself, but I'll look after you too."

"I like whisky." She pushed forward her glass with a hand bony, slightly dirty, tipped blood red. Norman half-filled it and poured the same amount in his own.

"It tastes all the better because it's freemans. Freemans from the Greek."

"That little bastard. There's only one thing he wants from the girls. And he gets it from some of them. Not me, though."

"You're too smart."

"I'm too smart."

She had finished that drink and started another before she began to talk. Norman had nothing more to do than sit in Nicholas' body-absorbent chair, a chair in a subdued, delicious blue that matched exactly the blue of his desk-top, nothing more to do than sit and listen. She talked in spurts, as water comes out of a hose that is intermittently blocked.

"Something was wrong, I could see that the moment they came in. King didn't look much different from the way he always does, mind you, went over and talked to that dough-faced Susie, but I saw from the way Ernie and Taffy went on that something was up. They're milky, those two, haven't got what it takes. The other one, Les Gardner, he's King's boy. I don't mean he's that way, you know, but King treats him as if he's sort of a kid brother. He's got a stuck-up bitch of a sister, Les, I mean, but he's all right himself, one of the boys.

"Now since King and I packed up – I told you we packed up?" Norman nodded, not wanting to interrupt her. "It was mutual, you understand that. Since then Ernie Bogan has been trying to make me. As though I'd look at that snotty-nosed kid after King. So he comes up and starts talking about something they've done out at Far Wether, not saying exactly what, talking as though it was something smart. Then King comes over, he hasn't said a word to me since coming in the place, mind you, but now he comes across and asks what Ernie's talking about.

"'He was telling me you went to the Guy Fawkes show at Far Wether,' I said.

"I've never seen King that angry. You know King?"

"I know King," Norman agreed.

"You know what he's like, cool as a cuke. Now he says to Ernie, 'I told you to keep your trap shut,' and Ernie says what about Rocky and the Pole, they're not here, and King says, 'Any bastard who says anything won't last long after this is over because I'll do him. You got that, Ernie?'"

The girl stopped suddenly, and looked at her almost empty glass. Her tongue came out, pink, and licked the red of her lipstick. "He could do it to me," she said in a voice from which the assumed Americanism had quite gone.

Now Norman felt the whisky he had drunk drain away, leaving him perfectly sober, and also felt himself becoming again, quite consciously, a detective sergeant, aware of his responsibilities towards society and even towards this errant girl. This was something that had happened to him before, as though he had been playing some monstrous game of "Let's pretend" that was now over; or as though he had gone deliberately to the edge, the very crumbling edge of a cliff and felt his foot slipping as the ground gave way, yet knew simultaneously that at any time he wished he could return to firm land. Now Detective Sergeant Norman, the lusts of the flesh and errors of the spirit put away, spoke with avuncular composure.

"He won't do it to you, girl. I can tell you one thing that's certain. At the end of all this we're going to put King Garney where he can't do anything to anybody for a long time. Now, what else did he say?"

"He didn't say much else, he didn't have to, Ernie was wetting his pants with fright. And then Taffy Edwards comes up and they're talking, but you know, kind of giggling too, saying it was fun. And I asked them what it was exactly that had happened, and Taffy said, 'King and Les did it. Ernie and me were there, but we never had knives.'

"'Did what?' I asked. 'Have you robbed a bank or something?' And then Taffy says they went out to have some fun with this bloke who chucked them out of a dance or something, and how they took a lot of fireworks to throw at him, but he got cut up. King and Les were the ones that had knives, Taffy says again.

"Then Ernie says, 'What about Rocky?' Maybe Rocky too, Taffy says, and Ernie says, 'You were flashing a knife before we went, Taffy,' and Taffy says he wasn't. So then I asked how bad they cut him, and Taffy giggles and Ernie says, 'Bad.'

"'How bad?' I said again, and Ernie says that King thinks he croaked."

Her glass was empty. She looked up. "Want another drink."

"You've had enough," said Norman, with a solicitude that had no more than a faint snail-smear of lechery left in it. "You come along with me."

She took his arm. "You'll look after me?"

"I'll look after you."

They went down to the station, and there she made her statement.

Chapter Fifteen

On Monday morning Hugh said, "I've got to go along to the station."

When Lane was in a good temper he smoked cigars. At times of annoyance he chewed cigarettes. His method of chewing was to light a cigarette, allow it to go out, roll it in his mouth until it was wet, and then chew the damp cylinder. He found the taste disgusting, and this exacerbated his bad temper. He was chewing a cigarette now.

"It's an identification parade. You know I was out at Far Wether on Thursday."

"Could I forget it?" Lane asked sweetly. "When you're not reading the *Banner* under the desk or writing stories for the other nationals which none of 'em are going to use, you're nipping out to have a cuppa with your friend Mr Fairfield. Shall I tell you something? If you don't pull your finger out and get cracking on a few little jobs for this paper instead of spending your time brown-nosing Mr Fairfield, you might not be coming back from one of those cups of coffee. Do I make myself clear to your great intellect?"

"Have I missed anything?"

"Did I say you'd missed something?" Lane spat out the shreds of his cigarette, dumped the mess in his ash-tray, and filled one of the pipes on his desk. A pipe was his emotional half-way house between cigarette and cigar. "This is Monday morning, boy. The arrests have been made, we've reported them, all right. Magistrate's court, trial, they're news and we'll report them when the time comes. But we don't want a *Gazette* reporter crawling round looking under every stone to see what's hidden. See what I mean?"

Michael stopped typing. "After all, there's the Savington Legion skittle meeting today. I mean to say, first things first."

"Very amusing," Lane said. "Extraordinarily humorous. And the funny thing is, our humorist is right. We're a local paper, and our readers come to us for local stories they won't find anywhere else. For a local story that makes national news they read the national press. Got it? All right. Now sod off and get your identification parade done and be back here by two o'clock."

A thin rain, soft and almost warm, dropped on him as he walked down the High Street towards the police station. He was the last to arrive. The lop-sided Joe Pickett, the lugubrious Dr Mackintosh, and the girl whose fireworks he had lighted, with a man who was presumably her father, sat on chairs in a waiting-room. There they were joined by Twicker, Langton, and a bulky, fleshily handsome man who was not known to Hugh, but whose name he gathered to be Norman. It was Langton, red-faced and slow-spoken, who talked to them.

"This is an identification parade. You four are going outside, one by one, and there you'll see several people. Look at them all – take your time, there'll be no hurry – and then tell us if you saw any of them on the green at Far Wether on the night of November fifth. We don't want anybody you saw before or afterwards, you understand that. We're just interested in any of them who were on the green that night. Do you understand?" There was a murmur of assent. Langton bent down to Maureen Dyer. "Do you understand, my dear?"

She whispered something. Her father said heartily, "Maureen understands. She'll do it, don't worry." Langton fumbled in his pocket and drew out a packet of fruit pastilles. He offered one to Maureen, who shook her head. Langton looked disappointed.

Now the three men left them and were replaced by Bob Pickering. They left the waiting-room in turn on being called by Norman, Dr Mackintosh first, then Maureen Dyer and her father. Joe Pickett said, "Seen you before. You're the reporter chap came out that night, aren't you?"

In a heavy voice Pickering said, "No talking, please." A minute later it was Pickett's turn, and a couple of minutes after that Norman looked in and said, "Mr Bennett."

They walked down the corridor together. In a rather loud, self-confident voice Norman said, "You're on the *Gazette*?"

"That's right."

"You had a nose for news last Thursday night. See how many of the boys you can pick out today."

They went out into a small courtyard. There twelve youths stood, all of them wearing raincoats or mackintoshes, all looking miserable. He walked slowly down the line and back again, but really the pretence at serious examination was a farce. Yet the farce had its disturbing aspect, for Gardner was his pigeon, and, curiously, he was now a little less certain about his identification of Gardner than when he had first suffered the shock of recognition on Saturday morning. It was upon that first shock, really, that he now relied, for, after all, what had he seen last Thursday night, what could he have seen in those seconds by the bonfire when his senses were not directed towards a particular identification? What could it have been, more than a momentary impression that might have been mistaken? For an instant the face of Leslie Gardner was overlaid completely by that of his sister, the snub nose and the short, appealing upper lip which were somehow not pathetic but expressive of determination, replacing the immature good looks of the youth who stood moving from one foot to the other uneasily, in acknowledgement of the journalist's prolonged scrutiny. It's all nonsense, Hugh told himself, of course I recognised him, it was absolutely instantaneous.

Twicker was by his side. The superintendent said formally, "Do you recognise any of them? Do you want to go down the line again?"

"No." Gardner flinched away from his nod. "This one."

Norman was making a note. "Yes?" Twicker prompted.

"He's the one I struggled with last Thursday. Then he broke away from me and went over towards Corby."

"Right. Say something," he said to Gardner.

The youth opened his mouth. "My name is Leslie Gardner," came out.

"Now say, 'Get him, King.'"

There was a flash of some emotion in Gardner's eyes. In the same blank voice he said, "Get him, King."

Twicker looked at Hugh, who shrugged. "I just couldn't say. Remember, these were only three words and I wasn't paying particular attention."

"Right," Twicker said. Norman put away his notebook. Hugh walked out of the courtyard.

Chapter Sixteen

The Chief Constable had lunched well, and was feeling cheerful. "What have we got?" he asked.

Twicker spoke, his voice dry yet not dull, a current of passion running clearly beneath it. Langton sat, stolid but attentive. Norman doodled on a pad.

"First, these five boys are under arrest. Their names are Bogan, Charkoff, Edwards, Gardner and Garney. A sixth boy, Jones, was questioned, made a statement involving two of the others, and has since run away from home." Twicker paused. Norman stopped doodling. Langton looked down at his big hands. The Chief Constable stroked his moustache. "There's no doubt that these six boys were involved in the earlier dance incident. No doubt either about their presence at Far Wether on the night of November fifth, which they have now all admitted after first denying it. The question is which of them were actually involved in the crime.

"Here we have four witnesses. Joe Pickett, a jobbing gardener, was standing close to Corby. Today he identified Garney and Gardner as two boys who actually attacked Corby. He saw a knife drawn, although he is not sure who used it. Garney, who is called King by the others, is the gang's leader, and it is natural to suppose that he would be involved. Pickett also identified two other boys as having been present. These were mistakes in identification." Twicker paused. Nobody spoke.

"Next, Dr Mackintosh, who was also at one time near to Corby, although he moved away. He agrees that Corby was attacked by 'two or three' boys. This morning he was only able positively to identify Garney.

"Third, an eleven-year-old girl named Maureen Dyer, the daughter of a local farmer."

"Old Jack Dyer," the Chief Constable said, "lives at Twelvetrees House, always used to have a fireworks party there every year. Wonder why he missed this year? Oh, sorry. Go on, Superintendent."

"Maureen Dyer identifies another boy, Gardner, as one who pushed her over. She says she saw a knife shining in his hand. She's quite sure she saw it. A local reporter, Hugh Bennett, also identified Gardner as the man who knocked over the girl. Bennett struggled with Gardner, felt something hard in his pocket, saw him move towards Corby."

The Chief Constable jingled coins in his own pocket. "I'd like to know where this Rocky Jones boy has got to. No news of him yet, eh?"

"Nothing yet, sir," Langton said. "But he won't get far."

"It's all rather confused," the Chief Constable said pettishly. "One saw this and another saw that. And then what about the boys themselves? I suppose they all tell different tales."

What does he expect, Norman thought to himself as he listened to Twicker recounting the different stories told by the boys, and then going on to an account of what Jean Willard had said. Did he think that the boys were going to serve it all up on a plate? A case like this was never easy, never cut and dried. At the end of this conference Twicker would make his report. It would be considered at Scotland Yard and passed on from there to the Director of Public Prosecutions, and the DPP would make up his collective mind. But you could bet your life that they would play it safe in a case like this and that one or two of the boys would be allowed to save their skins by turning Queen's Evidence. The question simply was, which ones? Rocky Jones, no doubt, when they found him, and that long-nosed Pole, Charkoff. It was damply warm in the room, with a gas fire hissing slightly, and Norman felt himself not sleepy exactly, but no longer following the discussion with full attention. There was a big leather armchair beside the gas fire. I bet he has his afternoon nap in that, Norman thought, looking at the Chief Constable's slightly vacant face.

"Sweat it out," the Chief Constable said. "Got to sweat the truth out of them, only way to deal with these types, eh?"

One of the three telephones on his big desk rang. The Chief Constable picked it up, spoke, handed it over to Langton. The superintendent spoke, mostly in monosyllables, for perhaps a minute, and then put down the receiver as if it had been a loaded gun.

"They've found Rocky Jones," he said. "He was in one of a couple of condemned cottages down by Platt's Flats."

"Good," the Chief Constable said heartily. "Get down to sweating a bit more out of him, get his tale straight."

"We shan't get anything out of him. He's dead. Someone did him with a knife."

Chapter Seventeen

Platt's Flats derived their name from a Victorian builder, who had erected upon flat marshy land two rows of cottages, with four rooms in each and a communal sewer. Most of the cottages had been pulled down but two remained, their roof leaking, their windows broken long ago and boarded. Photographs of band leaders and film stars were pinned to the damp and dirt-stained walls. Some empty beer bottles stood in one corner. There were three chairs in the room, and a cane-topped bamboo table. The body lay face downwards on the floor. There was a good deal of blood. Men were dusting with fingerprint powder, measuring distances, taking photographs.

"He's been stabbed eight times," the police surgeon told them. "Probably by two different knives, though it's hard to be sure, because if it was two knives they were both of the same flick-knife sort. No other blows struck that I can see, though I'll be positive of that when I've looked at him more carefully. It looks as though one of them held him and the other used the knife, then the one holding him helped to finish him off."

"There were two of them?"

The police surgeon was a professional pessimist. "Hard to be sure. Hard to be sure of anything. I'd have expected some sign of a struggle if there had been only one. But it could be that this boy, what's his name – ?"

"Jones."

"Jones, yes, it could be that Jones was terrified and just let one of them knife him. May have been one, two, or half a dozen for all I know. But I imagine your boys may have something to say about that."

"Time of death?"

"Oh, I don't know. Quite a while. Let's see, Monday afternoon now, suppose we said between ten o'clock Friday night and ten o'clock Saturday morning."

"He was under interrogation until midnight on Friday," Twicker said acidly.

The police surgeon was unruffled. "There you are. Shows how difficult it is to be exact after a couple of days. Mind, I may be able to get a little closer after the PM, but it will only be within six hours or so."

"Thank you very much."

"Glad to help. Any time."

Half an hour later they had been through the cottage. There were more beer bottles, together with bits of food, in the kitchen. The staircase was broken, and the upper rooms had not been used.

"How does this seem to work out?" Twicker asked. "Jones didn't run away as his father thought. That note he saw was one that called him to a meeting in this cottage, which was used by the boys. Once here he may have been questioned and given away that he'd sung to us. Or they may simply have known that he was the weakest link. Either way they killed him. It's the sort of thing Garney might do, making sure they were all there, so that the others kept their mouths shut."

Langton agreed. "That's about the strength of it. And if that's right we shall find the dabs of the whole gang all over the place, which won't help much in telling us which of them were in it."

There was a silence, broken by Norman. "The only way to find that out is to do what the CC said. Sweat it out of 'em."

Chapter Eighteen

Fairfield and Hugh were drinking in the Grand. Fairfield poured water into his pink gin, and drank half of it quickly. "Does your journalist's instinct tell you anything about what's going to happen now, young Hugh?"

"Reporters swarming down from London," he hazarded.

"That, yes. And the end of your pennies for linage. But this isn't a story that's going to send most editors into ecstasies, you know. A bit too sordid. That isn't just what I meant."

"Bad for Twicker?"

"Bad for Twicker. And Twicker's got one strike against him already, one at least. That's part of what I mean but not all of it. A thing like this happening generates a lot of pressure. The gods that be won't take any chances. They'll be out for blood."

He nodded to the barman and their glasses were refilled. Hugh protested feebly.

"Don't be absurd, my boy. The *Banner* picks up all these little tickets. Out for blood, I was saying. Heads will roll. They're going to have a case against some of these lads, and make sure that the case sticks. They'll turn on quite a lot of heat. Do you see what I mean?"

"Not really, no."

"I'll spell it out. From what I can gather they very likely won't be able to make the murder charge stick for the five of them, so they'll concentrate on some, and get the others to turn Queen's Evidence."

"I see."

"This gin's too pink," Fairfield said suddenly. "There should be only the faintest tinge of bitters, plop plop, two drops. Do you know angostura has an eighty per cent alcoholic content? Don't bother to answer, I'm talking to myself. But answer this. Do you suppose he's guilty, that boy Gardner? Is he the sort of boy who would use a knife like that?"

Did he think so or not? Remembering the figure breaking away from him and running towards Corby, he couldn't be sure.

"I don't believe he did it," Fairfield said. His jaw stuck out uncompromisingly, his face gazed into itself in the looking-glass. "Interesting chap, that father of his, good sound Labour type. And his sister, she's full of character too. With a father like that and a sister like that, he might be stupid and reckless, but I don't believe he's a murderer."

Hugh passed his hand across his forehead. It was hot in the bar. "I hope he's not. I like Jill. But what then?"

"If we agree, you and I, that he's innocent, I believe the *Banner* ought to put up the money to defend him. I think you and I ought to look around for anything that might be useful, that would help him, I mean."

Their glasses were filled again. Was Fairfield drunk, to be talking so wildly? His great ruined face was sober and severe.

"Aren't you putting the cart before the horse a bit? We don't even know that Gardner's going to be held."

"Garney is going to catch it. And this boy's his particular chum."

"Or that any of them will admit anything."

"*That's* better," Fairfield said, looking closely at his gin after adding water to it. "They'll admit things. This is a case that's going to generate an awful lot of pressure."

Chapter Nineteen

On Monday evening, and on into Tuesday morning, they sweated it out of the boys. Half a dozen of them did the work in relays. The interrogation now had two objects, first to get more information about the death of Corby, and second to get the boys to say something about the murder of Rocky Jones. Twicker took no part in the early questioning, and it was half past eight when Norman came in and said, "I've got Charkoff's statement, and I think we're through with Edwards. Shan't get any more out of them." The night was rawly cold, but Norman was sweating.

Twicker went with the Sergeant through a maze of corridors into a small room where Taffy Edwards, small and dark, sat shivering on a chair. There were two detectives in the room. Edwards' teeth chattered, and his colour was bad.

"Do you want a cup of tea?" Twicker asked.

"Yes." There were no marks on the boy's face, but he kept his hand pressed to his side.

Twicker nodded. One of the detectives got up and went out.

"Here's his statement, sir." Twicker read it. Edwards told the tale they had already heard from Charkoff about what had happened at Far Wether. Garney had suggested the expedition, and they had stocked up with fireworks. He had thought it was a bit of a lark, that was all. Garney often carried a knife, and had one that evening. He had seen

90

Gardner with a knife that night too, and he thought Charkoff had carried one. He admitted the conversation with Jean Willard in the Rotor, but said he had not actually seen the blows struck. When he said "King and Les did it," that was because they carried knives.

He agreed that they often met in the cottage at Platt's Flats, but persistently said that about the death of Rocky Jones he knew nothing at all.

While Taffy Edwards sipped his tea and nibbled at a thick sandwich, doing both with the slow delicacy of an invalid who returns fearfully to normality, Twicker compared this statement with the new one made by Charkoff, in which he said positively that Taffy Edwards was carrying a knife, and denied that he had one himself. About the death of Rocky Jones, Charkoff also said that he knew nothing.

Twicker said to Edwards, "This is all you know about the murders?"

"Yes." It was a whisper.

"And you made this statement of your own free will."

A shudder like an electric shock went through Edwards' body. "Yes."

"It's not satisfactory," Twicker said. "We know you had a knife that Thursday night. We've got statements that say so. And you know about Jones. You know who killed him, isn't that so? You'd better carry on, Norman."

"Yes, sir."

"Oh no, please. I can't stand any more. Please don't make them go on." Edwards began to cry. "I don't deserve this. Oh please, I don't deserve it."

"You've taken part in one murder, perhaps two." Twicker tore the paper on which the statement had been made, once and then again. "Now let's have the truth."

"I don't know what you want." Edwards held out his hands imploringly.

"When I say 'stand up,' sit down, and when I say 'sit down,' stand up," Norman said. "Stand up."

Edwards slowly rose.

"Why, you stinking little Welsh clot, don't you understand plain English?" Norman punched Edwards in the stomach. He sat down.

"I don't like this either." Twicker's face was severe and impassive. "But we're going to have the truth. You were carrying a knife on Guy Fawkes night, weren't you?"

"He's too big a cissy," one of the detectives said. "Wouldn't know what to do with it."

"Yes, he would," said the other. "He frightens babies in their prams. He's a tough little Welshman, aren't you, Taffy? Come on, aren't you?"

"I don't know."

"Say 'sir' when you speak to me. And stand up."

Edwards stood up. Norman slapped him on the face. "I didn't say anything, did I, stupid? You'll never learn. You had a knife with you that night, yes?"

"No."

"You were there when Rocky Jones was done."

"No. No."

"Stand up," said the other detective.

"Stand up. And I mean sit down," said Norman.

Edwards began to weep, helplessly, uncontrollably. Twicker turned away.

Just after half past nine Norman came to him, smiling. Edwards had made another statement, in which he admitted carrying a knife on Thursday night, and said that he had heard Garney and Gardner threaten Rocky Jones after they were all released.

"He's back in his cell now, feeling ever so happy," Norman said.

"He's all right?"

It was a question he should not have asked, but Norman did not show it. "Made of indiarubber. I'll see how the others are going. I think Bogan may be just about ready to sing."

When Norman had gone, Twicker sat, with a pen in his hand, looking at the wall. This was the way it happened, he knew that well enough, and it was foolish to wish that there were some other way. In his early manhood Twicker had felt himself a missionary working consciously for right and justice. Was it possible that they could be served by such instruments as Norman? In recent years he had come slowly and painfully to the belief that it was. He picked up the telephone when the bell rang.

"This is the lab."

"Yes." The laboratory had had the clothing worn by all the boys for examination, together with other jackets and trousers taken from their homes.

"Report on the clothes will be coming up officially, but I thought you'd like to have the gist of it now. Bogan, Charkoff Edwards, nothing to report. No bloodstains. Bogan's jacket is singed, presumably with fireworks. Now, Garney and Gardner. Garney first. He was wearing one of those leather zip jackets and the front of it's spotted with blood. Not just two or three spots, quite a lot. There are a couple of smears of blood on his trousers, quite big ones. All these are recent. We've tested them, and they're Group O. Corby was Group O. It's not Garney's own blood, he's Group A. There's a slight tear in the left trouser leg, near the knee. If you can find a convenient nail somewhere around it might be useful."

"I'll make a note of it."

"Now, Gardner. Wearing same sort of jacket, black instead of red. Bloodstains on it, quite significant ones, high up on the left-hand side of the jacket. Group O again. But, this is not so good, Gardner is Group O himself. It's the commonest group, you know."

"Yes, I do know."

"Sorry and all that."

"What about Jones?"

"Jones? Oh yes, he's Group O, too. No stains on trousers. Just one point about Gardner's trousers, though. Very nice smart gaberdine trousers, nicely pressed, newly cleaned by the look of it. There's an odd sort of dust in the turn-up, looks like coal dust mixed with something or other. Don't suppose it's important, but I'll let you have a detailed analysis."

Garney and Gardner, Twicker thought as he put down the telephone, it's always Garney and Gardner. He lifted the telephone again, put it down, and walked to the door. He had already been scathingly rebuked for releasing all the boys on Friday night. But on an occasion in the past Twicker had been too sure too early, and had suffered for it. He had released the boys out of a determination not to make the same mistake again. Undoubtedly it was now his duty to see Garney and Gardner in person. If they could not give a satisfactory answer about the bloodstains, well, they would have to go on sweating it out.

They went on sweating it out.

Chapter Twenty

The AC put down the report on the table. "Twicker seems to have put up a black."

"He certainly has," said his deputy, the commander. "And not for the first time."

The AC frowned. He respected Twicker, without exactly liking him. The commander, who did not share these feelings, drove the point home. "You have six boys who are obviously in this thing up to their necks. What do you let 'em go for?"

"Because you're not certain which ones were directly involved." The AC was conscious that it sounded feeble.

"They were all involved, it's plain as the nose on my face." The nose was plain enough. "I don't know what he thought he was doing."

"You want to take him off it?"

The commander said grudgingly, "He'd better stay on. I've given him a shellacking."

"Which I'm sure he richly deserves." The AC liked a quiet life. "The question is, what do we recommend to the DPP? You see the way Twicker's thinking?"

The commander used a toothpick expertly. "It's all damned thin."

"Oh, I wouldn't call it *thin*, exactly. We have, as you may say, considerable fire-power, but not sufficient to cover the entire front. We must choose our points for concentration."

The AC had, as he admitted, a weakness (but really he thought it a strength) for metaphor. "Now what I suggest is – "

His suggestion came in its time to the Director of Public Prosecutions and was discussed by two of the staff, one serious-minded and the other inclined to be flippant.

"Garney and Gardner were two pretty men. One said 'Let's do him' and the other said 'When?'" said flippant. "Garney and Gardner suggested and approved. Flopsy, Mopsy and Cottontail are good little delinquents and shan't have bread and water for supper. Agreed?"

"I'm rather worried about the whole thing," said serious. "It's true that we need those three as witnesses, and there really isn't a case to be put up against them, but somehow I don't like it."

Flippant sighed. It would be necessary, he saw, to chew over the case for the next half hour, to dot all the i's and cross all the t's and to deplore various aspects of Scotland Yard's handling and presentation of this and other cases. Fortunately he had three quarters of an hour to spare before lunch. "I entirely agree," he said. "But of course we've got to realise – "

At the end of these conferences the obvious conclusion was stamped and sealed. At the Magistrate's Court no evidence was offered on a murder charge against Ernest John Bogan, Vladimir Charkoff and Hywel David Edwards. John Allan Garney and Leslie Charles Gardner were committed for trial at the next assizes, on the charge that they had been jointly concerned in the murders of James Renton Corby and Frank Jones.

Chapter Twenty-one

Fairfield was never at his best, was never, indeed, happy at all, in Crawley's presence. It was not that Crawley lacked understanding or perception. On the contrary, he gave the impression of having already thought of, considered and rejected the idea that was being put forward, but of being nevertheless prepared to hear your final plea for it. Nor was it exactly that Crawley seemed machine-like but rather that, with his impassivity and his frozen smile, he had an air of being the god who operated the machine. And that he was, as it were, the personal representative of this god, Fairfield was well aware.

"Have you mentioned this idea to the boy's father?" Crawley said now.

"Not yet. There's a young chap named Bennett – "

"The reporter on the *Gazette*?"

"That's right. He's rather friendly with the boy's sister. Elder sister, twenty-two or -three, teacher in a primary school, a bit solemn but pretty. He's approached her about it. I think she'll play. Of course they were hoping that the case would be thrown out in the Magistrate's Court, but now the boy's been committed." Fairfield coughed. He had come back to London on the previous night and done a lot of drinking, and his throat was parched.

There was a glass of water on the table and, as Fairfield coughed again, Crawley lifted the glass, took a single sip, and replaced it. "There are no other children? Two or three years old, something like that?'

"No. Mrs Gardner died of cancer five years ago."

"Pity." Crawley was referring, Fairfield knew, to the lack of small and appealing children. "And the father?"

"A real dodo, left wing, local councillor, ambitious for his children, thinks we're the agents of the devil." A grin spread over Fairfield's battered face, but it received no acknowledgement. "No money. He might turn us down flat but I don't think so, not if his daughter gets to work on him."

"Yes. What's Bennett like?"

"Bennett? Nice boy, young but bright. He's been a lot of help. I like him."

Crawley had made one or two notes on the pad in front of him, using a very hard pencil which wrote with scratchy neatness. He was silent for a few seconds, and then Fairfield felt the cold touch of his smile. "Thanks very much, Frank. I'll let you know something during the day. Be around, will you, unless there's something urgent."

Those seconds of consideration had led Crawley to the conclusion that the idea did not justify a special call to Lord Brackman. It could be kept as a titbit for his daily discussion.

When the catarrhal voice with its background whine of permanent dissatisfaction came on, however, it spoke for five minutes about the iniquities of patent medicine manufacturers.

"Got a lot of stomach trouble, Edgar. Bowel trouble. Want something to keep me regular and nothing does it. I go once in four days. Why don't we do something about it?"

"What's that?" Crawley had failed to follow this train of thought.

"Expose these frauds. Take a teaspoonful of this or a tablet of that, guaranteed to keep you regular. That's what the advertisements say. *They don't do it,* and our job as a responsible newspaper is to say so." Brackman very nearly cleared his throat to launch another volley of speech, but remained disconcertingly silent.

"I think we should be careful, Brack. Fighting this kind of war doesn't help anybody." Crawley's criticisms were so rare that Brack often paid attention to them, but he did not care for contradiction.

"What have you got for today?" He spoke sharply.

Crawley endured a running fire of hostile remarks in relation to his handling of half a dozen items. Was this an unfavourable time to mention Gardner? Perhaps not.

"The Guy Fawkes murder," he said. "You've seen that Garney and Gardner have been committed?"

"Yes. The story's finished. Kill it until the trial."

"Fairfield thinks there's a chance that Gardner's father might agree to our backing the defence of his boy. If we want to run a crusade, that is." This was well put. The idea appeared to be Crawley's own, yet it was still easy to transfer responsibility for it to Fairfield.

There was no sound but that of Lord Brackman's catarrhal breathing. Then he spoke. "Tell me about it, Edgar."

Crawley told him what he had learned from Fairfield. His narrative was punctuated by grunts, and at the end of it there was another hard-breathing silence. In moments of emotion Lord Brackman tended to speak in monosyllables, and he did so now. "I like it, Edgar. I like it. I think it's good."

"Yes, Brack."

"What I like," said Lord Brackman, his words slow and thick as treacle, "is that this chap's Labour. Show's we're straight. We don't care how he votes, don't care who he is. We're for the little man. We want to see he gets a chance. And when it's a lad like this… "

Crawley waited until it became evident that the sentence was finished, or was to remain unfinished.

"Yes, Brack?"

"Edgar, I want you to come over. We'll talk about this. Come and have lunch. 'Bye."

Crawley put down the receiver, took off his thick glasses and polished them. His eyes, without glasses, could be seen as pale, small, watery. He spoke to his secretary, and told her that he would be with Lord Brackman.

During these conversations the question of Leslie Gardner's guilt or innocence had not been mentioned.

Chapter Twenty-two

This was a provincial city, near the mouth of a river. There was a good grammar school and a fine hospital. There were four streets with shops in them which were, as everybody said, as good as any London shops, and these streets led off the square in the centre like spokes off the hub of a wheel. Walking down them you could remain unaware of the docks and canning factories upon which the city lived. The city had two good restaurants, one of which stayed open until ten o'clock, and in the past twelve months three Espresso bars had been opened. Hugh Bennett sat in one of these bars, the Just a Sec, with Jill Gardner.

"Dad and I went to see Leslie today. I've never seen him so miserable." He said nothing. "Have you heard from Frank?"

They both called him Frank by this time. "Yes. He rang the office. The *Banner* wants to do it, to pay for the defence."

She sipped her coffee. "I can't make up my mind. Whether it's a good thing, I mean. Though it's really up to Dad."

"Frank wanted us to go along and see him. It will mean a better counsel. I'm sure it must be worthwhile. Try to persuade him." He hesitated. "Of course, it will mean a lot of publicity. You know, pictures of the family, personal articles and so on. And then they want the option to buy Leslie's story."

"If he's acquitted, you mean."

"What's he like, Jill. Really like?" Hugh was always to have the sense that he never pushed beyond the outer skin of reality, and he was vividly aware that this was not, could not be, all there was to know. If one could push below this flexible yet resilient skin, twitch it aside as one takes the skin off custard, surely there must be some ultimate truth in the liquid depths below? So he asked himself, what are they *really* like, the people caught up in these events? What circumstances made them as they are? It seemed to him that if he could understand this, he would have penetrated one of the secrets of life itself.

"Did Leslie help to kill them, do you mean?"

That was not what he had meant, or no more than a fragment of it.

"I don't know. But if he did I blame myself, myself and Dad." The corners of her mouth turned down.

"Don't." He put his hand across the veined table-top, so that it rested on hers.

"It's all right. I shan't cry, I never cry. There was a boy who wanted to marry me a couple of years ago. He was going out to Rhodesia and I wouldn't go. 'You're just a meat and two veg girl,' he said to me. 'That's you, Jill, and that's going to be your life.' And he was quite right, don't you think?"

"I shouldn't think so. But anyway, it doesn't matter."

A waitress was standing over them, listening avidly. "Eight o'clock. We're shutting."

They went out into the streets of the city, where it seemed always to be raining, the soft rain of autumn that made the few cars now moving around the city centre suck and lick at the shiny black roads. Hugh Bennett walked along the streets beside the shut shops in a trance of gentle pleasure, his hand occasionally and as if by accident touching Jill's, while she talked about herself and about the past.

"You remember what Frank said that night, the way he talked to Dad. In a way he was right, I expect you'd say he was right, but he was wrong too. Dad only wanted us to be good people, Leslie and I, that was all, he was only doing the right thing."

"What he thought was the right thing."

"What else is there?" She wore a red plastic mackintosh with a white hood, and now she turned and looked at him in surprise. "Dad says you've got to live with your circumstances, whatever they are. There's no use trying to get away from them. What you are, the condition you grew up in, is something you carry around all your life."

He recognised another voice behind the words. "What about the way your brother grew up?"

"He was the sweetest kid, Leslie I mean. Eyes the same colour as mine, a sort of blue grey, but much bigger. And so pretty. Quick at learning. He's still only a boy, you know, only seventeen. I don't understand, I just don't understand what went wrong with him. I suppose it's since Mother died. She spoiled him, you know, let him do what he wanted. He was never any good at school after that, always saying he wanted to have a job and earn money. He was at the grammar, but he left before he was sixteen. It changed Leslie's life, Mother's death, can you see that? In a way everything was the same, we stayed in the same house and all that, but still it changed our lives. It was after Mother died that he started going about with Jack Garney."

"Tell me about Garney."

"He's the eldest of seven children. His father's a Roman Catholic, works in the docks, good money, knocks his mother about." Her mouth was drawn into tight, disapproving lines. For an instant she looked like her father. She saw his glance at her, and laughed. "Don't I sound awful? That's what it does to you, being brought up in Peter Street, you're on one side or the other. Either you're part of the Garneys and the Joneses or else you're against them, that's what it does."

103

"That sounds like a good argument for not living in Peter Street."

"In some ways any place is pretty much the same," she said defensively. "You can call it snobbish, but there are grades of snobbery everywhere. I see lots of them in school. You must remember them from your own childhood."

"Not really. My father was killed on D-Day when I was seven. He was a sergeant in the Armoured Corps."

"I'm sorry."

"Why be sorry? It's a long time ago."

"And your mother?"

"She was always bored with me, I think, and my father's death was the last straw. She arranged for me to go to stay for a holiday with Aunt Millie, my father's sister. She lived twenty miles out of the city, in a village called Parmile. I was to stay while my mother got a new job, and then she'd come down to collect me. It was a long holiday."

"Your mother didn't come down?"

"It was awkward, you can see that, my mother got a job in London and thought I ought not to be exposed to flying bombs and all that. Eventually I was shunted off to an inferior boarding school. I went on living with Aunt Millie."

"But that's terrible," she cried. "Simply terrible. I don't see how she could have done it."

"My mother? I used to think that, but I've got over it now. She married again. I see her twice a year." He could talk about it calmly now, without remembering too clearly the terrible feeling of absolute loneliness he had endured so long ago. Her next words astonished him.

"Very good for you, I expect."

"Oh no." The memories came flooding painfully back. "Not good for me or anybody, how can you say that?"

"It would have been good for me. To be alone, no responsibilities, you don't know how I long for it. But I suppose a meat and two veg girl always has responsibilities, whether she wants them or not. Here's our tram stop."

"Tram stop?"

"You want to see Dad, don't you? We'd better stand inside here, we're getting awfully wet."

They stood in the doorway of a closed toyshop and he looked at the train sets, the soldiers, the cowboy suits, the parlour games, all the apparatus of childhood that he had missed through the lack of love and the restrictions of war. Her face was turned away from the toyshop window and as she stared out into the wet street he divined behind her softness of voice and feature something hard, not flexible. She took off the white hat, shook it, and turned to him smiling.

George Gardner sat in the kitchen eating a piece of veal and ham pie with pickle. A coal fire burned in a small grate, and the room was warm. He kissed his daughter, nodded to Hugh, and went on eating, cutting up the pie into small pieces and dabbing each piece deliberately into the pickle.

Jill shook herself. "How was the meeting?"

"All right. Jill, pour young Bennett a cup of tea, there's some left in the pot. And yourself. What's the news?"

"Hugh's got something to say to you," she said as she poured the tea.

Gardner listened as he talked about Fairfield's idea, listened, cut up the pie, speared the pieces and dabbed them into the pickle. Then he took an apple from a plate of fruit and peeled it deliberately. When Hugh had finished, Gardner took a drink of tea. He finished peeling the apple, cut it into four pieces and removed the core from each piece with one brisk motion.

"That all?"

"That's all."

"Why didn't your friend Fairfield come down and say it himself? Afraid I'd send him off with a flea in his ear, I suppose. So you're the Trojan horse."

"He's up in London. I don't think there's any other reason."

Gardner ate a piece of apple. When he spoke, Hugh was dismayed to hear in his voice the rhetorical tone he used for public meetings. "So you're suggesting that I should let the *Banner* pay for the defence of my son on this charge that's been trumped up against him. Let's consider for a minute, and see what everyone's going to get out of it. I can see what the *Banner* gets, clear enough. A lot of good publicity, some articles by their sob-sisters who say what a rough life we live in Peter Street, how bad conditions are and all that. All going to show this is a slum district and you can't live decently in it, undercover propaganda against the Labour movement which I happen to represent. And what do I get? What do you think the people round here are going to say, people who've voted for me and put me on the council when they hear about me being financed by a Tory newspaper?"

In a perfectly even voice Jill said, "Put a sock in it, Dad."

"What?" He stared at her, brows drawn together. "What's that?"

"You're not standing trial for your principles. Leslie is, for murder."

Gardner sat at the table, which was covered with red and white plastic, one big hand gripping the cup of tea, staring at her. "You mean you want me to accept? You want our pictures in the paper, is that it?"

Jill would always argue with her father, Hugh realised, in this cool conversational tone, but the words she spoke were no less direct and wounding than his. Listening to her saying things that he could never have said himself, he sensed the tug of love and distrust between these two. A meat and two veg girl could never have any use for rhetoric.

"I just want you to think about it from Leslie's point of view, that's all. Just for once, don't worry if people say you're selling out to the Tories. Suppose it helps to get Leslie off, does that matter? How are we going to pay for his defence?"

"The union might help."

"The union." She laughed.

"And anyway, he can choose from the counsel in court. There are always some there, isn't that right?" He appealed to Hugh.

She sat down and put her elbows on the table. "Do you mean to sit there and tell me that the counsel we'll get under the Poor Persons' Defence Act or whatever it is, will be as good as the one the *Banner* will get for us?"

"You don't believe he's innocent, then? You think he did it." He got up with his plate and cup, and took them to the sink. Back to her, he said, "I'm sorry, girl, I shouldn't have said that."

"It doesn't matter. Leslie's in prison now because he went around with Jack Garney. And why did he choose to go around with Garney? I've got something to answer for, but my word, Dad, you've got a lot more. Isn't it you that said the conditions you grow up in are something you carry around all your life?"

He swung round, his face naked, hurt. "Jill, you know I've always tried to do the best I could."

"Trying wasn't enough." He stayed silent. "Another thing. When Leslie comes out he's not going to be able to stay round here. The *Banner* wants an option on his story. Whatever the money is – how much do these papers pay?" she asked suddenly.

Hugh was taken aback. "I don't know. Five hundred pounds perhaps, or it might be as much as a thousand."

"Do you think Leslie will thank you for saying no to it?"

"It's not easy, Jill, not as easy as you make it sound."

"It's easy to me," she said. "Either you think about yourself or you think about Leslie. It's as easy as that."

"I think I ought to go," Hugh said hurriedly. He felt that he could have borne shouting more easily than her even-toned argument.

In the draughty, narrow, dark passage outside, she said, "You see what I mean about having responsibilities?"

"I suppose so."

"He's got to do it, though. I'll see that he does it." They were very close to each other. He put out a hand and gripped her arm. The flesh was plump and yielding. Her lips brushed his in the coolest and slightest of caresses, and then she murmured good night. He was out in Peter Street, which was dark and wet, and seemed unnaturally silent.

On the following morning she telephoned him at the office to say that her father had agreed.

Chapter Twenty-three

From the *Daily Banner*, 10th December:

FAMOUS QC FOR DEFENCE IN GUY
FAWKES CASE
Magnus Newton briefed by *Banner* to defend
Leslie Gardner

Today we announce a sensational new development in the Guy Fawkes case, in which two boys, Leslie Gardner and John Garney, are to be tried for the murder of landowner James Corby on 5th November, and of Frank "Rocky" Jones, a key witness who was found murdered in a deserted cottage on the morning of 9th November.

Mr Magnus Newton, QC, who has appeared for the defence in several of the most important murder cases of the past decade, including the La Perouse trial, the Wilkins case and the Sydenham poisonings, has accepted the brief for the defence of Leslie Gardner. Mr Newton is probably the most highly paid counsel at present in criminal practice. It is estimated that his income for the past five years has exceeded £25,000 per annum. The whole of the costs of the defence will be paid by the *Daily Banner*.

Lord Brackman, proprietor of the paper, said in announcing this yesterday, "The whole problem of juvenile crime is of vital importance in our modern society. It is in pursuit of my belief that the accused should have the benefit of the finest counsel available that my paper has agreed to bear the costs of the defence, and I am delighted that Mr Magnus Newton, whose eminence at the criminal bar is universally recognised, has found it possible to accept the brief. There are no political issues involved here. The *Banner* is concerned simply that justice shall not only be done, but shall be seen to be done."

Lord Brackman was no doubt referring to the fact that Mr George Gardner, father of the accused boy, is well known as a Labour councillor. Last night Mr Gardner said, "I don't agree with the *Banner* politically, but I am grateful for the generosity that has led them to sponsor my son's defence."

(Pictures of the Gardner family at home, and a profile of Magnus Newton, on page 6.)

In fact, the briefing of Magnus Newton had been almost entirely Edgar Crawley's work. It was Lord Brackman's habit to originate schemes, leaving the details to others. Just as Crawley had adopted Fairfield's idea as his own, so Brack had adopted Crawley's, and just as Crawley had sketched an alibi for himself by mentioning Fairfield's name, so Brack in conversation linked Crawley's name with the defence of Leslie Gardner – not as its originator, certainly, but rather as an obstacle whose in some ways admirable caution had to be overcome by Lord Brackman's verve and tact. This deceived nobody, yet it was a precautionary measure that allowed Lord Brackman to go into the enterprise with an easy heart, and he put himself at one farther remove from the actualities of the situation by quite refusing to say what counsel he wanted to engage.

Crawley, for his part, built defensive barriers by getting advice in writing from the paper's Legal Department, and by approaching first of all Sir Godfrey Challon and Athelstan Vickers, both of whom he knew to be far too busy to take on the case. These were feeble enough defences, to be sure, and nobody was better aware than Crawley that there is no real defence against the accusations of a superior, yet they put something on the file.

Opinion in the office was not favourable to the briefing of Magnus Newton, nor in fact to the scheme itself. "Your boy's had it now," Banks of the Legal Department said to Fairfield. "He's a regular kiss of death, Newton. Never got an acquittal yet in a murder case."

"There always has to be a first time," Fairfield said cheerfully.

"But not this time. Mind you, the boy's guilty as all get out, I'm not saying that even a good criminal lawyer could get him off, but with Newton you've just about hammered the last nail in his coffin. Hold on, though, he's only seventeen, isn't he? So it won't be a coffin, but just detained during Her Majesty's pleasure."

"I don't like your taste in jokes."

"Still, you've made a nice little stunt out of it. What are you working on now?"

"I'm going back. There's a lot of work to be done before we've finished."

"And when will that be?"

"When he's acquitted."

111

Chapter Twenty-four

For Hugh Bennett these weeks of his association with Frank Fairfield were always linked with the wet, mild fogginess of that winter, a fogginess so persuasive that the reporters' room of the *Gazette* was always filled with a faint mist. It seemed to be through this sort of slight fuzziness that he saw Fairfield's face. They met and talked always, or this at least was as he remembered it afterwards, in bars, in the American bar of the Grand or the station, the Shades at the County, the saloon bars of a dozen other pubs, most commonly the Goat, which was used by several people from the *Gazette.* And it seemed also, in retrospect, that Fairfield never ate anything more than an occasional sausage or sandwich, although he drank all the time. He drank large pink gins for choice, but among inveterate beer-drinkers he would drink beer too, pouring pint after pint down his throat with no apparent effect beyond, at the end of an evening, a slight further glazing of his vague eyes. He always said that the drinks were on the *Banner,* and the *Gazette* reporters, accustomed to having the shillings of their expense account questioned by an acidulous female accountant, were deeply envious of the largesse in which they shared.

"Do you know what your friend Fairfield is?" Michael asked one day. "Just a soak. Pure and simple. I do really rather *despise* that."

"I don't honestly see how that man Fairfield holds down his job," Clare Cavendish said after one session in the Goat. "I mean, he drinks all the time, and he doesn't seem to be *doing* anything."

It was Farmer Roger, however, who was most outspoken. One day, after they had drunk with Fairfield until closing time, he walked a little unsteadily back to the *Gazette* and asked Hugh to come into the little cubby-hole that served him as an office. Here, flanked by the *Farmer's Journal* on one wall and the works of Surtees on the other, he stroked his blue chin with a well-kept hand, and spoke like a patriarch.

"I've watched your progress in this office, young Hugh, and I've thought, there's a boy who'll go far, a lad who's got the real stuff of journalism in him and is still aware of life's richer realities. Life has a natural rhythm, my boy. The surge of the life force is not to be found on city pavements." His hand waved the air, he hummed a little.

"I don't know what you mean."

"A boon companion, I don't doubt, your friend from the great wen, but beware of thinking he is anything more. A man without roots, Hugh, a drifter on the sea of life, a scavenger fish feeding greedily on the misfortunes of others, the parasite inhabiting the shark." He hiccuped. "You see my similes are not confined to farm and field."

"Nor your inventions."

Farmer Roger looked at him drunkenly. "I beg your pardon."

"It wasn't true, was it, the story you told me about Mrs Corby and Weddle?"

Farmer Roger ran a hand through his curly grey hair. "It sometimes amuses me to embroider the plain cloth of fact with the golden thread of fancy. But my general thesis is incontestable. It can be put, indeed, as a syllogism. Your Wesleyan Presbyterian steeple-hatted sort of psalm-singer is randier than my prize bull Braggart. Weddle is a Wesleyan Presbyterian steeple-hatted psalm-singer. Hence Weddle is randier than Braggart."

"There wasn't a word of truth in it now, was there?"

Farmer Roger hiccuped again. He said gravely, "All my words are words of truth."

He could not now even be annoyed by Farmer Roger's evasions, but was left wondering how the witty profundities that had once enthralled him could have changed so utterly to the interminable ramblings of a club bore. Slowly his attitude towards the whole office altered, so that Lane seemed no longer a cigar-smoking omnipotent ogre but a failure bolstering self-importance with a loud voice, and Michael's talk of mares and poppets appeared not fashionable as he intended but an echo of what had been fashionable the year before last, and Clare's desperate striving for modernity stamped her somehow as incurably second-rate. All these things came about through his association with Frank Fairfield, yet they did not come through anything that the crime reporter did or said, and certainly not through any criticism he voiced of the *Gazette* or its staff. He seemed content to stand for whole evenings or lunchtimes at a bar, buying drinks and taking desultory part in the conversation, smiling occasionally at some private joke. He never voiced again the criticism of provincial journalists that he had made on that first evening in the flat. Yet this battered man, his raincoat wrapped round him like a flag, seemed to Hugh an epitome of some odd sort of journalistic integrity.

"You know, Hugh," he said one day, "you're one of the biggest bloody stumbling blocks we've got. Are you absolutely certain you saw Leslie that night?"

He had been over and over this in his mind. The image of Leslie's face (they both now used the Christian name in speaking of him) seen in that flare of green fire, and then seen again outside the house in Peter Street as he dashed unavailingly for freedom, had become almost inextricably mingled with the face of his sister, but he was bound to say, "Yes."

"And then you felt this something hard in his pocket which might have been a knife. It might have been fifty other things too, even if it was Leslie. You know he denies it."

"Yes."

A face seen in the light of a flare, some object momentarily felt and tentatively identified, it was upon a dozen such things that a boy's freedom depended. Fairfield voiced something of his thoughts.

"It's all very circumstantial, you know, the case against Leslie. If he hadn't been a friend of Garney's, I doubt if they'd have tried to pin it on him. All cases are circumstantial in a way, but I've seen the depositions, and I wouldn't say this is strong. These bad boys who turn Queen's Evidence are never liked by juries. Not but what I should say Garney's for the high jump anyway. It would be a good thing if we could get them tried separately."

"What are the chances of that?"

"About sixty-forty against, I should say. But what we really want is some defence witness who would say that all the identifications made on the night of November the fifth were so much baloney (begging your pardon, Hugh), because it was too dark to see your hand in front of your face, something like that."

The words revived a memory. "There was a chap in a duffle coat. A chap who said he'd seen the whole thing, but it was too dark to identify anybody. What was his name, now? Morgan."

They went out to Far Wether in a car which Fairfield had hired, and which he drove with disturbing insouciance. George, the landlord of the Dog and Duck, knew Morgan. "Chap as always wears an old duffle coat, long-faced chap looks as if he needs a shave. Yes, he lives up the road a couple of mile, Pebwater Farm, can't mistake it. Red brick tumble-downish sort of place."

"He is a farmer?"

This caused some amusement. "That's what he calls himself," one of the regulars said. "Leastways, he's got a farm."

"A bad farmer?"

"He's tried all sorts, Morgan. On to mushrooms now."

The gate of Pebwater Farm was open, but the house appeared deserted. When they had thundered on the knocker for the third time the door suddenly opened. A woman stood there. She was in her late thirties, a lush beauty gone to seed. She wore a grubby housecoat and satin slippers. Her hands were well shaped, and the red nails were immaculate.

"Mrs Morgan? Can we speak to your husband?"

"He's doing the mushrooms." She made a gesture towards three disused railway carriages some thirty yards away from the house. "What do you want?"

"I'm from the *Banner*. My name is Fairfield. This is my colleague, Hugh Bennett."

"Oh." She said flutteringly, "If you'll wait just a moment I'll come and help you find him."

They waited ten minutes, and then she came out wearing a coat and skirt, and with freshly applied lipstick. They went into two of the carriages. The fungi sprouted in their beds of mould, but they saw nobody. "Would be the last, wouldn't it?" she said with a bright smile. Before they reached the door of the third carriage it opened, and a man came out. Hugh recognised him at once.

"Darling, these gentlemen are from the press," Mrs Morgan said with delicate suburban refinement.

Morgan did not look at them. "You left this door open," he said, pointing to the door behind him. "Last night."

The red-tipped fingers went to the red mouth. But she was not really disturbed. "I certainly did not."

"The crop's done for." He said, not to anybody in particular, "You've got to keep them at an even temperature."

"The door must have blown open."

"That's the profit on a week's growth, gone like that."

"Oh, please, darling, don't let's wrangle. From the *Banner,* I think you said, Mr Fairfield?"

"And what do you want?" Morgan asked gloomily. "If you're looking for someone to tell you farmers are feather-bedded, you've come to the wrong man."

"Shouldn't we just go inside and talk about whatever it is over a nice cup of coffee?" Mrs Morgan's laughter gaily and meaninglessly trilled.

Women's magazines had overrun the living-room. They were piled in heaps beside the window and on tables, and littered singly on chairs. A chair sagged and creaked as Fairfield sat in it. "You'll have to forgive me," Mrs Morgan said. "I've had just no time to tidy. Now, in half a jiffy I'll have the coffee ready." They had a glimpse of a kitchen cluttered with dirty plates and saucepans, and Hugh saw with astonishment that the women's magazines, like some science fiction monster, had crept out to the kitchen too.

"It's about the Guy Fawkes night business, I suppose. I've told the police already. I couldn't say anything that was any use."

"But we're not the police. My paper, the *Banner,* is backing Gardner's defence." Fairfield made a gesture to Hugh.

"I was there on that night myself," Hugh said. "You were there too. I heard you say you were standing by and that it was too dark to see anything."

"That's right. I was a few yards away, mind."

"And later in the pub, when Joe Pickett said he'd recognised two of them, you said it was dark and he couldn't have seen a bloody thing."

"Here we are." It was Mrs Morgan again, with four cups of steaming liquid and a plate of biscuits on a tray. The liquid was not coffee, but one of its synthetic substitutes. "Have you been able to help the gentlemen, darling?"

Morgan ignored her. "I coulda been mistaken."

"Or Pickett could have been mistaken," Fairfield said.

"I'm a man that's used to speaking my mind. Always have, always shall. But I wouldn't have said what I did about Corby asking for it if I'd known they stabbed him. Caused a bit of bad feeling, that did. What I say, would you print it in the paper?"

"No. We'd get the defence solicitor to come out and see you, take a statement. Then you'd give evidence at the trial."

"Nothing in the paper," said Mrs Morgan disappointed.

"You keep out of it," her husband snarled. "You've done enough, leaving the shed door open."

"If you want to see Joe Pickett get away with it, all right."

"I don't want to see anybody get away with anything. I don't want to run into any trouble, either."

"It was too dark to see faces?"

"For me or Joe Pickett, yes. I know where Joe was standing, couple of yards from me."

"It's up to you," Fairfield said with apparent indifference.

Morgan crunched a thin rich tea biscuit, took a mouthful of liquid, and said savagely to his wife, "This ain't coffee. If you ain't going to make coffee, why don't you say so?" He walked deliberately to the window, pushed aside a pile of magazines, and emptied the contents of his cup on to the garden.

His wife burst into tears and ran to the door. There she turned to them, a face ravaged with tears, and said, before she vanished, "Excuse me."

Morgan faced them. "I'll do it. You can send out your solicitor. I'll stand up there in court and say what a bloody liar Joe Pickett is."

When they drove away they heard the sound of weeping from an upstairs room.

Chapter Twenty-five

The sense of liberation, of a horizon slowly widening, that came to Hugh Bennett through Fairfield, did not extend to the activities of Fairfield's colleagues on the *Banner*. The crime reporter gave the impression of being somehow detached from the two photographers and the girl from features named Sally Banstead who came down. Sally Banstead was a girl smarter than paint, with a trim figure, a lively look, and every single strand of hair on her neat head perfectly in place at nine o'clock in the morning. Sally Banstead drank whisky, but she was not a drinking girl, and when she came to look for Fairfield in the Goat or in the Grand, as she sometimes did during her three days in the city, her undoubted respect was mixed with a sort of vague impatience. The impression she produced was not so much that she did not understand people like Frank Fairfield, as that she lacked time for the solution of a puzzle that was of no practical use.

"There goes a woman on her way to the top," said Fairfield once as she left them in the Grand, walking away with a step brisk but unhurried and a buttock-waggle that was both feminine and entirely impersonal. "And she'll get there, you know, she'll get there. If that's what you want, Sally's the kind of person to be." He suddenly sang in a voice ludicrously cracked, "'I know where I'm going, and I know who's going with me.' But personally I should say the man who's going with our Sally won't have an easy ride." He lifted his pink gin with that slightly trembling hand, and drank.

Just where Sally Banstead was going and what she was doing he learned from a rather chastened Jill, when she came in one day to the Pile Street flat.

"It was really awful, Hugh, the way they went on in Peter Street. If I'd known what it was going to be like I'm not sure that I'd have told Dad to accept. It's like – I don't know what it's like, but Magnus Newton had better be good, that's all."

She told him the kind of thing that he had heard about but never seen. Sally Banstead had been assigned to get interviews with all the families involved, and to get pictures. The Bogans had refused to talk or to provide photographs, and Sally had abstracted a photograph of Ernie Bogan from the front parlour while Mrs Bogan was explaining just why the family didn't want to be interviewed. She had asked Garney's father such personal things that he had chased her out of the house, whacking at her with a stick. One of the photographers had taken a picture of Garney standing at the door with the stick raised, and Sally had revenged herself by raking up all the details of his misdemeanours.

"We weren't popular in Peter Street before, but our name really stinks now. We shall have to leave, even Dad says so."

"How has he taken it?"

"We knew what we were in for ourselves, and we didn't mind that, even though it was so silly. She asked me about my boyfriends, and they've played up Dad being politically opposed to the *Banner* and my being a teacher – how Dad was determined to keep his children respectable. But I expect you've seen it." She shivered. "Why does it have to be like that, journalism?"

He had no answer. "How's Leslie?"

"Oh, I don't know. When we see him he never says anything, just says he's all right and stares at us. I don't think he wants us to come at all." She looked at the floor and then up again. "I'm not crying. I told you, I never cry."

He put his arms round her and they kissed, lovingly but without passion. Her last words were about Sally Banstead. "She's a real horror, that woman. I knew people like that existed, people without human feelings at all, but I'd never met one."

Fairfield shook his head when Hugh told him this. "She's wrong there, Jill. Sally's not exactly a machine, she looks after her father and mother. Her father's blind and her mother's partly paralysed, but they don't want to go into a home and she won't send them to one. She pays for someone to look after them all the time."

"But suppose this happened to her? Suppose somebody came in and forced them to give interviews and stole photographs, what would she think?"

"She'd be upset. But she'd go on doing the same thing herself. You can't change life, you've got to accept it." On this same evening he went on to talk, as though there were some logical connection, about Twicker. Fifteen years ago, he said, Twicker had been the youngest detective superintendent in the CID, a man marked out by his intelligence and devotion for advancement. "The thing about Twicker is that he really hates crime and criminals. He's not just a chap doing a job, he feels real passion about it. He's absolutely honest, you could never even suspect him of taking dropsy, he's got no personal vanity like a lot of them, he's truly devoted to the idea of justice."

"An ideal police officer."

"I didn't say that." Fairfield went on with his story. A man named Weston had been suspected of murdering a girl. Twicker had been in charge of the investigation. There had been a good deal of evidence against Weston, but not enough to justify his arrest. Twicker had been certain of Weston's guilt, and the fact that this murderer remained free infuriated him. He made Weston's life a misery in all sorts of obscure ways, ensured that his landladies knew that the man who'd taken a room with them was still under suspicion of murder, had unofficial visits paid to a whole series of people who gave Weston a job, so that they knew just what sort of man was in their employ. Weston lost job after job, moved from place to place when landladies found suddenly that they wanted his room. He complained, but Twicker had covered his tracks too well for the complaints to be effective. At last he gave in. He went to his local police station and said that he wanted to see Detective Superintendent Twicker and make a confession. In Twicker's presence Weston confessed to the girl's murder, and added a good deal of detail about things like throwing the murder weapon into a ditch nearby. The ditch was searched and no weapon found, but Weston was arrested. In due course he came to trial.

"At his trial Weston said that the confession had been made only so that he could prove his innocence. He had been subjected to intolerable persecution. He wanted to clear his name fully and finally, so that at last he would be a free man. He said that the confession was untrue in every detail.

"There was no decisive evidence against him beyond the confession. The Judge, before the opening of the defence case, advised the jury that it would be unsafe to convict. The jury acquitted Weston without leaving the box."

"And Twicker?"

"He'd been made a fool of. He's never really recovered from it."

"Would you say that was why he let those boys go when he ought to have held them?"

"I expect so. He'd made his mistake. He wasn't going to make the same sort of mistake again."

"Mistake's a kind word for it. He'd been persecuting an innocent man."

Fairfield stared. "Not at all. Twicker and everybody else on the case knew Weston had done it. Three years afterwards he killed another girl and was hanged for it."

Chapter Twenty-six

In the third week of December the weather became still milder, damper and foggier. Fairfield and Sally Banstead had gone back to London, with the reporter from the other nationals. They would return again, most of them, for the trial in January, but until then the case was wiped out of their minds. Hugh spent a hectic three quarters of an hour with Frank Fairfield drinking in the station bar, before the crime reporter caught his train.

"Don't forget, Hugh, if you come across anything at all that might be useful to Leslie, let me know. I'll be down on the next train."

"What does Magnus Newton think about it?"

"The likes of me aren't allowed into the councils of the mighty. It's said he's very hopeful." He sipped his drink and lit a cigarette. "Providing Leslie's been acquitted, will you feel it's all been worthwhile?"

He stared. "Of course."

"And your girlfriend?"

"I'm sure she will."

"She's a girl of character, that one, she reminds me of my second wife. But whether it's wise to marry a girl of character, I'm not so sure about that. How about her father?"

"How about him?"

"Our infantile Leftist, the Labour councillor who doesn't like the *Banner,* what does he think about things now?"

"I don't know. He's pretty cut up about all the publicity, they don't love him any better in Peter Street for it. But if everything comes out right he'll accept it."

Fairfield finished his drink, turned his blurred gaze upon Hugh and, as often, appeared about to make some profound remark. In fact he said, "You can't make omelettes without breaking eggs. Goodbye, young Hugh."

He picked up his bag and was gone. Hugh felt, to his surprise, a sense of loss.

A couple of days later he went round to Peter Street to have supper. They ate grilled chops and drank beer. George Gardner hardly spoke, and it was not a comfortable meal. At the end of it he said to Hugh, "Your friend Fairfield gone back to London?"

"Yes."

"Finished picking the bones and gone with the other vultures."

Jill was washing up. She banged a saucepan on the sink.

"She doesn't like my saying it. She thinks I ought to be grateful," Gardner said.

"I don't say grateful. It was a sort of deal, wasn't it? We knew what we were doing."

"I didn't know what it was going to mean," he said heavily. "I didn't know old Slattery, who's been a good Labour man all his life, was going to say he'd vote Tory at the next council election or that Bogan, Fred Bogan, that layabout, would say I'd been stirring up trouble for the whole street."

"You can't help what they say." To Hugh she said sharply, "You can dry."

"But it's true. I have caused trouble for the whole street. That bitch pinching a photograph out of a house. Do you justify that?" he said to Hugh. "Does your friend Fairfield justify that?"

126

"You knew what it was like," Jill said. If Michael could have seen her now, Hugh reflected, he would not have said she was a poppet or anything like it. "If you didn't know you should have done. You've talked enough about what the capitalist press is like."

"When you get it done to you and the people you know, it's different."

"Don't think about yourself so much. Think about Leslie a bit more. You don't suppose I like what they say at school, do you?" She wiped the bowl and said to Hugh, "Let's go out."

When she had put on her coat she came back to the kitchen. Gardner was still sitting at the table. She patted his shoulder. "Cheer up, Dad. We're in for it now. No use crying."

In his upward look Hugh Bennett saw behind the face's fine façade weakness and doubt. "I expect you're right."

In the street she said, "I feel sorry for Dad, don't think anything else. But showing it doesn't do any good."

"We can't always help that, can we? Not doing any good, I mean."

"Then we ought to. Not to be able to control your feelings, that's feeble. I've always admired Dad because he was so strong. Now, I don't know."

They went to the flat in Pile Street and he made coffee. Before she went to catch the last tram back she kissed him fiercely. "I'm sorry I'm so awful. I'll be better later on, when this is over. We shall get him out, shan't we?"

"We shall get him out."

At the office also the Guy Fawkes murder dwindled into insignificance. Hugh had one conversation with Grayling in which the editor, with a good deal of plate-clicking, referred again to the excellent stories that had been done on the case. Mr Weddle felt, he said, that the whole thing had been handled with admirable discretion. Now we must get back, mustn't we, to the more humdrum affairs of every day? Hugh, who had spent part of the afternoon at a Christmas bazaar organised by the Townswomen's Guild and opened at some length by the wife of a local MP, refrained from saying that he had got back long ago.

There was no chance of forgetting that Christmas was upon them. In the space of one week he attended seventeen different bazaars, fairs, jumble sales and sales of work, organised by various churches, British Legions and local shops. He suspected Lane of putting him through this agonising experience deliberately, and Michael and Clare of enjoying his frantic leg-work. The friend of the great London reporter was being shown his exact place in the *Gazette* hierarchy. But he did not complain even when Lane, yellow teeth bared, complimented him upon the niceness of his touch in handling this sort of thing.

"You've regularly got the Christmas spirit," Lane said in great good temper. "Never known a lad so full of Dickensian jollity. Does my old heart good to read paragraphs of true Christmas cheer."

Clare gave an uncustomary giggle. "He does do it rather well, doesn't he?"

Lane looked at her appreciatively. "You've got a new hair-do."

"Do you like it? Maurice in Pickard Street did it. He's really rather good."

"I'm so glad," Lane said, in a parody of her voice. "Because Maurice is doing the hair of one of our city's typical housewives, forty-eight-year-old Mrs Jackson, at three-thirty this afternoon. It's a special demonstration of the new Crispa brush cut, or that's what it says here. Will you just toddle down there and get an interview with Mrs Jackson. And with Maurice, too, if he has anything to say."

"Oh, my God." Clare picked up her notebook, banged her desk and went out.

"As for you, Hugh, my boy, just to vary the routine, there's a Religious Training Centre out at Welby which is having a sort of passing-out parade this afternoon. Let's have a piece of your deathless prose about that, will you."

He took his raincoat off the peg and went out to Welby. For the first time he admitted to himself that he was bored with life at the office. He said as much to Michael that evening, over supper in the flat.

"You're suffering from London fever. I told you not to get any ideas."

"Do you really think so?"

"Honestly now, didn't you dream about being offered a job in London?"

"Perhaps I did. But not seriously."

"We've all done it, my boy, we've all done it." Out of his greater experience Michael sighed. "I remember how excited I was when the *New Statesman* printed a piece of mine about local reps. I had visions, I dreamed dreams, I went up to London. I was given a book to review, a book on theatre, five hundred words. I wrote the most dazzlingly witty piece you can imagine, sweated blood over it. And do you know what happened? A printers' strike. My review never even got into proof."

Hugh sighed. He had heard the story, with slight variations, several times. "Perhaps you're right."

"Of course I'm right. You can forget about the Guy Fawkes murder. It ran into some nice linage, that's all. Shall we go out and have a drink on that?"

"If you like." He would not admit, even to himself, how bored he was, with what vague, eager expectancy he looked forward to the trial in January.

Chapter Twenty-seven

Just a week before Christmas, Magnus Newton came down from London in the company of the defence solicitor, Charles Earl of Earl, Sheldick and Partners. They sat in a private sitting-room at the Grand, waiting for George Gardner and his daughter. Magnus Newton stumped round the room on his little legs, took one glance out of the window at the gleaming wet streets and said in a grumbling voice, "The father's a red-hot Labour councillor, is that right?"

"I believe so." Looking at the two one would have thought that Earl, elegant and darkly handsome, was the barrister. Newton was short, puffy, red-faced, and appeared chronically irritable. In cross-examination, however, he used this irritable manner to good purpose, giving an impression of just managing to contain himself in the face of impenetrable stupidity, which often put a self-confident witness out of his stride. At times, however, Charles Earl found himself wishing that Newton would reserve his petulance for cross-examination. He had maintained a sort of subterranean grumbling about various aspects of the case all the way down in the train.

"We certainly don't want politics drawn into this affair, it's messy enough already. Still, if he's a councillor I suppose it means the boy was well enough brought up. What time are we due to see him?"

"At four o'clock."

"I'm glad I've got a thick overcoat, it's damned cold in prison. Damned cold in here for that matter. Why don't they have a decent coal fire instead of these filthy radiators?"

The solicitor knew perfectly well the reason for Newton's annoyance. Very few counsel nowadays care to interview a client they are defending on a murder charge. They prefer that the solicitor should act as intermediary, remaining themselves detached from personal contact. But in this case the *Banner* had insisted or, rather, had conveyed through the assistant editor, Edgar Crawley, the wish of the proprietor, Lord Brackman – that Newton should visit his client. There was a *Banner* photographer in the hotel now who would take pictures of George and Jill Gardner in conference with Newton and Earl, a picture of barrister and solicitor at the prison gate, and pictures of them visiting Far Wether and Platt's Flats. It would make a picture feature, and Newton was a glutton for publicity. At the same time, he accepted the whole thing with a bad grace.

There was a knock at the door. Earl said with some relief, "Here they are." As the Gardners came in he nodded to the man who had brought them up and said, "Five minutes."

As he shook hands with the Gardners, Newton summed them up. The man a typical working-class figure, ill at ease in his best suit. A fine head, though, good broad shoulders, a look of awkward honesty. Upon the whole Newton was favourably impressed. The daughter was pretty enough, in an unpretentious, unfashionable way. Newton, who liked flamboyant beauty, paid little attention to her.

They had been talking for a little while when the photographer came in. "Is it all right now?"

Earl said, "All right."

"If you'll sit a little closer. Mr Newton in the middle talking to Mr Gardner."

Newton brushed away the ash that always collected on his waistcoat. Gardner stood up. "What is this?"

"This gentleman is from the *Banner*," Earl said. "He's here to take pictures."

"This is just another publicity stunt, then?"

"Certainly not. They're simply taking a couple of pictures, that's all."

"Taking a couple of pictures. What have they been doing ever since it all started but taking prying pictures, poking their noses into other people's business? I'd like to break his bloody camera." Gardner took a step forward. The photographer retreated. "I thought this was to be a serious conference about my son's case. Seems we're just jumping through the hoops again when the *Banner* cracks the whip. I'm not doing it, that's all. Either he clears out or I do."

"Mr Gardner." Newton stood with his head thrust forward, a little red-faced bullock about to charge. "You made this arrangement with the *Banner*."

"Yes. But I never knew what it would mean."

"You made the arrangement. You knew it would entail personal publicity, just as Mr Earl and I knew it. If you don't want to abide by the arrangement, say so. Mr Earl and I will withdraw from the case." Gardner glared at him. Newton went on remorselessly, "If you wish us to go on acting in your son's interest, sit down."

Gardner sat down and folded his arms. "Take your pictures."

The conference lasted twenty-five minutes. There was really little to say. Afterwards Earl congratulated Newton. "I thought you handled him very well. He's an awkward customer."

Newton puffed a little. "Trouble-maker. I know the type. But respectable."

"What the girl said about the boy being timid was interesting, useful perhaps."

"Yes. Though you've got to be careful about these things. If we make much of that, very likely it'll turn out that he enjoyed sticking knives into dead birds or something. Let's have a look at Master Gardner, shall we?"

They went to the prison in one taxi and the photographer followed in another. He took a couple of shots outside the prison gate, of Newton bare-headed in the rain looking pensive, with Earl, briefcase under arm, standing by his side. Then Newton and Earl went inside.

Newton saw the boy alone, in a tiny room with two chairs in it. Leslie Gardner was very pale, and looked less than his seventeen years. The main points of his story had already been established, but Newton ran over the details again. On Thursday night he had gone to Far Wether and had thrown fireworks. He had not knocked over a little girl and had not struggled with a young man. He had not shouted, "Get him, King." On the following night, Friday, when Rocky Jones was killed, he had been released by the police at the same time as the other boys, and had come straight home and gone to bed.

"Now, about the bloodstains on your leather jacket. They're your own blood group, Group O. Have you any idea when you made them?"

"Must have been sometime during the week." Gardner muttered the words, and did not look at Newton as he spoke them.

"You can't identify it more exactly than that? It must have been some occasion when you were out on your motorcycle, I suppose. Or did you wear the jacket indoors?"

"Hardly ever wore it indoors, no."

"Might it have been lying about indoors when you cut your finger, so that some blood got on to it?"

"Might have been, I s'pose."

"You can't remember?" Newton cursed himself for letting the conversation get into this channel. Such a reaction as he was now getting from Gardner created exactly the kind of impression that a barrister does not want to have left in his mind.

" Can't remember, no."

"If you do remember anything, get in touch with Mr Earl at once. It may be very important to you. You understand that?"

He thankfully left the point. "Now I want to talk to you about Garney."

For the first time the boy looked animated, even excited. "King's smashing. He's been smashing to me."

"You've been influenced by him?"

"Everyone has, everyone he knows. Anything you can think of, King can do it better than anyone else. I've seen him jump off a twenty-foot wall just like that, it's all a matter of the way you land, he says. And he can throw a knife – " He stopped suddenly. Newton coughed.

"This is what I'm getting at. Would you say that in your – " he tried to think of a synonym that would avoid the use of the word *gang*, at last said weakly – "in your group, you were his best friend?"

"Sure. King and me are like that. He's got no time for some of the others, the Pole for one. They're just hangers-on, sort of."

Newton spoke clearly and slowly. "The prosecution – that is, the other side – may try to make you say that you admired Garney so much that you would have done anything he told you."

Leslie Gardner's eyes flickered at him and away.

"For instance, that you might have held the boy Jones while Garney stabbed him. That may be put to you. But you don't look to me like the kind of boy who'd do anything another boy told him. Your father and sister brought you up differently to that."

"I hate him."

"What's that?"

"Jill's all right. I hate Dad." Now the boy stared boldly at Newton. "He's always on at you. About education and work and all that. Wanted me to stay on at school. I'd had enough of it when I was fifteen. Before then, as a matter of fact. I mean, they treat you like kids."

"I see."

"What I mean is, he's all the time talking at you like you were a public meeting. For your own good and all that. I never asked to be done good to. Why can't we live like the others do in Peter Street, I asked him, why do we have to be so different, why was he afraid I'd disgrace him? Jill was a bit that way, too, but you could get round her. She's human."

"I've seen your father today. You know he's made these special arrangements for your defence?"

"I never asked him to." The boy lapsed into apathy, then said, "What about King? Who's defending him?"

"That's not my business, I'm afraid," Newton said stiffly. He found Leslie Gardner, in his way, even more infuriating than his father. "Don't forget about the stains on your jacket, that's important."

When he rejoined Earl, the two walked in silence through the prison courtyard. "A bit raw, isn't he?" the solicitor said. "And inarticulate. But not really stupid."

"He hates his father and worships Garney. When I told him his father had made special arrangements for his defence, he wanted to know who was defending Garney."

"Good afternoon, sir," said the man on duty at the gate.

"Good day," Newton said with unnecessary violence. On the way back to the hotel in the taxi he said to Earl, "Ghastly weather, ghastly city, ghastly people. I wonder there aren't more murders here."

On the following day he was photographed on the green at Far Wether. A swirling mist spoiled the effect of the slightly Napoleonic attitude in which he stood looking at the scene of the bonfire. Another photograph was taken at Platt's Flats, with Newton pointing at the cottage and talking earnestly to Earl. Then the barrister and the solicitor went back to London.

Newton spent Christmas at his home in Hampton Court with his wife and their only child, thirteen-year-old Viola, who had a friend to stay from school. He and his wife bought Viola a dozen presents, one less than her age. They knew they were spoiling her, but found it impossible to break the habit. Newton sang a lot of comic songs in a husky baritone, and enjoyed himself very much.

Hugh Bennett spent Christmas Day with his aunt. He saw Jill on Boxing Day and gave her a wristwatch as a present. She gave him a tie. She had gone to visit some relatives of her mother on Christmas Day. Her father, she said, was very gloomy.

Twicker stayed at home with his wife, who was a semi-invalid. A couple who lived in the same road came in, and the men played chess while the women talked.

Norman took his girl to have Christmas dinner with his family, and at about eleven o'clock the two of them went on to a party which lasted until six o'clock on Boxing Day morning. He woke at half past nine, without a headache.

Leslie Gardner and Jack Garney stayed in prison. When Garney refused to eat the Christmas pudding, first of all telling the warder exactly what it looked like, Gardner also refused to eat it.

Chapter Twenty-eight

It was on his return to the office after Christmas that
Twicker made the discovery that was to draw the net round
Leslie Gardner so that it was suffocatingly tight. Nobody
knew better than Twicker that the case against Gardner was
– not thin, exactly, but a case in which almost every detail
was a supposition, resting upon the evidence of accomplices
who were intent to save their own skins, or upon
incriminating things said in the hearing of a girl who,
according to Norman, was not much more than a tart, or
upon things seen in the doubtful glare of a firework. This
sort of confusion is a frequent concomitant of a murderous
scuffle, but there is often one piece of quite unassailable and
damning evidence that clinches all the rest, and puts a jury's
possible doubts at ease. It was just such a piece of evidence
that Twicker felt to be lacking in relation to Gardner. And to
the bitter passion that the superintendent felt always against
criminals, his frustrated sense that all of the boys were
equally guilty and should have been charged as such, was
added the practical knowledge that his mistakes had been
such that he could not afford to fail.

It was with such thoughts in mind that Twicker sat in his
office looking at the sample of dust that had been taken from
the turn-ups of Leslie Gardner's trousers. He remembered
what the analyst had casually said: "Very nice, smart
trousers, nicely pressed, newly cleaned by the look of it."

And of the dust he had said that it was odd, seemed to be some sort of coal dust. It had proved to be odder than that. The specks were almost equally brown and black, and the full report said that they appeared to be compounded of fine coal dust and silver sand mixed together. Where did one find silver sand? In a builder's yard, on a building site. But that was of little help, or no help at all. Twicker had a vivid visual memory, and he summoned up now the green at Far Wether, the burnt-out patch that had been a bonfire and the grass surrounding it, lush, coarse and wet. No trace here of coal dust, no trace of sand. How could there be? He took out this slide from his memory and replaced it by the interior of the cottage at Platt's Flats. His mental eye carefully examined the cottage, front room and kitchen, and then the rooms upstairs. The floors were dusty, no more than that. Outside, then? Outside there had been a good deal of mud, the way to the front of the cottage had been muddy. There was certainly no building work going on there. Move round the cottage, then. What was round at the back? Twicker suddenly exclaimed out loud.

That afternoon Twicker and Norman went down to the city together. They took with them that pair of nice, smart trousers, pressed and cleaned, and the sample of dust found in the turn-ups. Norman did not share the excitement expressed in Twicker's eagerness of movement and gesture. He had no objection to being out of the office for an afternoon, but thought or indeed felt sure, that they were on a wild-goose chase. A police car took them to Platt's Flats, and beside the two ruined cottages Twicker jumped out, no longer a battered veteran but a young terrier hot after a reluctant bitch. For once it was not raining, but as they got out of the car their feet squelched in mud. Norman, following his too-impetuous chief, bent his mouth down in distaste. His shoes were becoming uncommonly dirty.

138

Twicker ignored the front door, bored round the right of the cottage and reached the back. He said triumphantly: "There." Norman also stood gazing.

At one time each of the Platt's Flats cottages had had its own garden, a tiny square patch of green with a rudimentary path to the back gate. The back gates had gone, the little gardens had merged into each other and become one single wilderness, but there remained an occasional distinguishing mark like that outside the cottage in which Rocky Jones had been found. Children had lived here, loving parents had made a sandpit with a load or two of silver sand. It was the remains of this sandpit that they were looking at, an area enclosed by boards, and still retaining a relic of its former use in the shape of a small toy spade. Beside the sand there had been a coal bunker. They lifted the bunker's top and saw that it was now almost empty. The wooden bottom of the bunker had been sapped by rain and had given way, so that fragments of coal dust had run down and mingled with the sand. Twicker bent down and began scooping the blended sand and coal into a polythene bag. Then he spoke.

"He came in the back way that Friday night. Perhaps he always did. As he came in it was very dark and he walked through the sandpit. No doubt he got the stuff on his shoes too, but he must have cleaned them off, forgotten the trousers."

"Perhaps," Norman said. "It depends when they were cleaned."

"That's what you're going to find out. We should have done it before, but there didn't seem any point. If you can do it without the Gardners knowing, so much the better. First of all find out what laundry they use. Go along there and take the trousers with you, see if they keep a record of stuff sent in for cleaning, I think most of these laundries do. If you get nothing out of the laundry, try the dry-cleaners in the neighbourhood."

"Right."

"One pair of trousers, nicely pressed, newly cleaned by the look of it," Twicker said. "One old sandpit, one load of coal. If those trousers had really just been cleaned, they may be exactly what we've been looking for."

There are times when everything seems to go exactly right, when all the difficult things come easy, and each penny drops into its right slot. Norman found out from Taffy Edwards' family, who lived farther up Peter Street, that the Gardners used the Kwick-N-Clean Laundry in Lamb Avenue. The manageress of the Kwick-N-Clean was wonderfully helpful.

"We collect from the Paradise Vale area each Saturday and deliver again on the following Friday," she said. "And there's a separate record made of every cleaning job. Of course they go down in the laundry book too."

"Have you got the Gardners' laundry book?"

She hesitated. "I expect so. You want to see it?"

"I do." Norman's glance was conspiratorial. "And this is between you and me. I don't want anyone else, anyone at all, to know about it."

"I understand." She was a demure, not unattractive, fat woman. When the book came with its label, *Gardner, 24 Peter Street,* she handed it to him without a word.

Norman turned up the entry for Saturday, 31st October. It was written in a neat hand which he guessed to be Jill Gardner's, and at the bottom of it he read, "For Cleaning. One pair grey trousers." He said, with rising excitement, "This item, the trousers, would have been returned on the following Friday, 6th November?"

"That's right."

"And there would have been a separate entry made out for them here?"

"For all cleaning items, I told you. They're separately charged. You want to see the copy of the job slip?"

He said that he did. She came back with a book which she opened out before him. "Here you are. These are the carbons of all the cleaning work. This is the one. Name, Gardner, 24 Peter Street. Article, pair grey trousers. Job Number 41622. Now the next heading is 'Van or Shop' and that means it has been either delivered by the van or collected. You'll see it says 'Van.' Date – that's the date of van delivery – 6th November. Sixty-three, that's the number of the girl who did the cleaning work. There you are."

"Is there any way of checking this particular pair of grey trousers? These are gaberdine trousers. Can we make sure whether or not this is the pair that came in for cleaning on 31st October?"

She shook her head. "We don't go as far as that, putting down whether they're gaberdine or not. A pair of grey trousers is just a pair of grey trousers."

He thought for a moment, then went carefully through the Gardners' laundry book for the last two months and found that nothing had been sent for cleaning except a raincoat. He said to her, "You've lost this book."

"Now, just a minute."

"You've lost it," Norman said firmly. He put the book in his pocket. "You can say so, and issue them with a new one, can't you? With apologies, of course."

" I suppose so. Is it really important?"

"It's important." Norman sat on the edge of her desk and smiled at her. "And here's something else important. I don't want anything known or suspected about the way this laundry book got lost. You look to me the sort of girl who can keep a secret." She simpered a little at being called a girl.

"I am."

"Then mind you keep this one. If I hear that it's been getting around I shall be very angry." He placed a hand on her plump arm and pinched it sharply.

"It all fits," he said, when he got back to Twicker. "Gardner had them cleaned on 31st October, they came back on 6th November, so he can't possibly have worn them before then. Therefore he wore them that night. We've got young Gardner where we want him."

Twicker showed no emotion. It had been a smart idea, Norman admitted that ungrudgingly, but it somehow took the edge off his own pleasure that the super didn't show surprise or any trace of pleasure, but simply said, "Yes."

"What do we do about it?" Norman asked, although he knew very well. Twicker stared at him. "I mean, have we got to let them know? This is something that's really going to rock them."

Twicker did not even answer, did not even trouble to remind Norman that all evidence material to the case discovered by the prosecution must be made available to the defence. But it is possible to hasten slowly, and it was not until three days before the trial that a document headed "Notice of additional evidence" arrived on Magnus Newton's desk, and the barrister read with concern that "Charles James Norman, sergeant in the Criminal Investigation Department, will now additionally swear... " From Newton this news of additional prosecution evidence filtered through to Edgar Crawley, and from Crawley to Frank Fairfield.

Chapter Twenty-nine

The *Daily Banner,* 11th January:

GUY FAWKES TRIAL BEGINS TODAY
TWO YOUTHS ACCUSED OF DOUBLE KILLING

The public gallery was full when Frank Fairfield and
Michael Baker walked into the Assize Court, showed
their cards and found places behind the little barrier
that said *Press.* It was with the most unctuous mock-
sorrow that Lane had told Hugh that, since he was to be
called as a prosecution witness, it would naturally not
be proper for him to be in court before he gave evidence,
and that in view of all the circumstances the editor had
decided that Michael should report the proceedings. It
was reasonable enough, but Hugh could not escape the
feeling that Grayling and Lane and even Michael, who
professed to find the whole thing a bit of a bore, took
pleasure in his exclusion. On the day that the trial
opened he spent the morning at Welby Petty Sessional
Court and took notes on eight traffic offences, three
arrears of maintenance cases, one indecency charge and
a common assault. He was not forgotten, however. At
precisely ten-thirty Michael leaned across to Frank
Fairfield and murmured, "Pity poor Hugh."

The two prisoners had entered the dock, Garney dark and self-assured, Gardner slight and pale. The Clerk of the Court rose. "John Allan Garney, are you guilty or not guilty?"

"I am not guilty," Garney said in a strong, clear voice.

"Leslie Charles Gardner, are you guilty or not guilty?"

Gardner's voice was dull. "Not guilty."

The clerk sat down. Magnus Newton was on his feet. Mr Justice Beckles looked at him severely over the top of his half-spectacles, and said in a squeaky voice that conflicted with his ruggedly handsome face, "Yes, Mr Newton?"

"My lord, I appear on behalf of Gardner. I have an application to make on his behalf, a most important application from my client's point of view. It is that your lordship should order a separate trial in this case... "

"Here it is," Fairfield whispered. "You can sit back for an hour."

And in fact it was for fifty-five minutes that Newton spoke in his melodious boom, referring to the conflicts of evidence that existed, the points that would be made by various witnesses against first one of the accused and then the other, the prejudices against Gardner that must inevitably arise if his case were to be heard with Garney's. Fairfield sat with hands on the desk in front of him, making an occasional note. His attention wandered to where Jill Gardner sat with her father just behind counsel, wearing a dark blue coat and skirt, her face very pale. Now Newton was quoting his authorities, turning to the marked places in one book after another. Mr Justice Beckles squeaked an occasional interrogative interjection. "The matter is within the judicial discretion," Newton wound up, "but in view of all the circumstances to which I have called your lordship's attention, I pray that your lordship will make an order that in this case the accused should be tried separately."

Newton sat down abruptly. In a moment Gavin Edmonds, a dapper, mottled man in his forties, who represented Garney, was on his feet.

"What's he like?" Michael whispered.

"Good enough, but lightweight," Fairfield whispered back. "Makes a speciality of attacking the police. Gets the headlines but doesn't do much good, especially in a murder case."

Edmonds spoke in support of the application, in a dry, clipped voice that contrasted strongly with Newton's. It was a fear that Garney's case might be prejudiced through association with Gardner's that was in his mind, it seemed, and he began to quote his own authorities. The Judge showed signs of impatience, and Edmonds spoke for only twenty minutes. Eustace Hardy, who was leading for the Crown, rose slowly. Mr Justice Beckles peered at him over the spectacles.

"I don't think that I need trouble you, Mr Hardy." Eustace Hardy was very ready to sit down again. "An application of this sort is often made on the ground that there has been mutual recrimination of one prisoner by the other, or that what one says will incriminate the other. That does not apply in this case, and it seems that the two accused are close friends. It is said that there is a conflict of evidence, but this is for a jury to decide, and the mere fact of a possible conflict of evidence cannot be accepted as a reason for granting separate trials, in which the great mass of evidence referring to both defendants would have to be repeated before two juries. In my opinion no sufficient reason has been shown for making the order, and I must refuse the application."

"First blood to them," said Fairfield. There was a scraping of feet in the public gallery, a shuffling of papers in court. Newton leaned over in earnest consultation with his junior, Toby Bander. Jill Gardner looked once briefly at her brother, smiled and looked away. Her father sat with hands on knees staring at the Judge in wig and robes.

Now Eustace Hardy was on his feet at last, and speaking in a voice which was quite unlike the clipped tones of Gavin Edmonds or Newton's fine but monotonous boom. He had what is still sometimes called a silvery voice, beautifully delicate and clear, a voice which was quite plainly recognisable, by those who cared to recognise such things, as the product of a particular public school and a particular university – even, as some claimed, of a particular college at that university. The jury, naturally, made no such act of recognition, but they understood instinctively that Hardy represented something alien to their own way of life. There was a sort of effortless superiority in his manner, a quite unintended air of talking down to those beneath him in the social and intellectual scale, that had stirred deep prejudices against him in many juries. Against the prejudice often raised by his manner could be put his extraordinary lucidity of exposition, the incisive intelligence of his mind, and his quite deadly skill in cross-examination. The credits outweighed the debits by a long chalk, but the debits undoubtedly existed.

"The night was dark," Hardy was saying, "but the scene was illuminated by the bonfire and also by a green flare – that is, the flare of a firework – which was burning at this time. There was quite sufficient light for anybody who was standing close beside Corby to see who attacked him. You will hear that Joe Pickett, a local gardener, saw three boys attack Corby, and identified the prisoners as two of them. You will hear Dr Mackintosh, who also saw the attack, and who identified Garney. You will hear Maureen Dyer, a young girl whom Gardner knocked over before he moved on towards Corby, and a local reporter named Bennett, who grappled with Gardner and later identified him. In deciding which of the boys stabbed and murdered Corby, these witnesses are of vital importance.

"And it is important also, ladies and gentlemen, to consider the behaviour of these six boys after the assault. Four of them went to a dance hall called the Rotor that evening, and you may feel that their conversation and the admonitions, or even threats, used by Garney, who was by common consent their leader, are instructive... "

"Not a good word, admonition," Michael whispered to Fairfield. "Half of them don't know what it means."

Fairfield did not look up. He was making notes. Michael made a face at him and began to take notes himself.

"...We do not know what was in the note which, according to what young Frank Jones said to his father, was left for him after he reached home that Friday night. But we know that Frank Jones was frightened by it, and told his father that he would run away. Yet he did not run away. Perhaps he was too frightened even for that. He went instead to keep an appointment in the deserted cottage that was used by the boys as their headquarters. He was killed in that cottage, brutally stabbed to death. He suffered eight stab wounds, inflicted by one or more hands.

"Now, ladies and gentlemen, according to the medical evidence Jones was killed between midnight on Friday and six o'clock on Saturday morning. The boys did not reach home after their interrogation by the police until past midnight, so that the time of the murder was in the early hours of Saturday morning. I do not pretend to have traced the prisoners' movements at this time, when it would be natural to suppose that they were in bed and asleep. I will say frankly that we have no witness who saw them in the vicinity of the cottage. But I shall present what is, I believe, irrefutable evidence – evidence based on laboratory research into Gardner's clothes and on the investigations of Detective Superintendent Twicker and Detective Sergeant Norman –

that Gardner was at the cottage that night. On that night, ladies and gentlemen, and not on any other night. That means, if you will bear in mind the times I have already given you, that Gardner was present when Jones was murdered."

Hardy paused for a moment and then continued, moving on to another point. Could it be said that there was anything like a sensation in court? Hardly. Mr Justice Beckles, above them all in his red robes, placed a hand over his mouth and stifled, ever so delicately, a yawn.

Chapter Thirty

"May we join you?" Fairfield asked, for him a little formally. He had bought a sandwich at the pub counter, and had a glass of beer in his other hand.

"It's a free country," Gardner said.

"I know you don't like me."

"It's not you. It's the paper you work for." He made this response in an imperfectly audible voice.

"His teeth," Jill said. "He broke his plate this morning. It had fallen on the floor somehow and he stepped on it."

It was possible to see now that Gardner's whole face had caved in, leaving the cheeks gaunt and hollow, the whole expression curiously changed. When he cut a piece of the pie on his plate and pushed it about in his mouth, the effect was somehow pathetic.

"I wanted to talk about this question of the grey trousers. I expect you've had the defence solicitors along to see you. Ah, here's Hugh."

The Petty Sessional Court at Welby had yielded only two paragraphs, one on the assault and another on one of the traffic offences, in which a well-known local tradesman had been found guilty of exceeding the speed limit in a built-up area, and also of driving with a faulty speedometer.

"How's it going?" Hugh asked.

"Only just begun. What about the trousers?" he said to Jill.

"Somebody came along from the solicitors. But I couldn't explain. I just don't understand it. Leslie says he doesn't understand either."

"Leslie went straight to bed that Friday night and slept till morning," Gardner said indistinctly. Fairfield ignored him.

"Now look, the police never asked you about this, did they? So they must have got their information direct from this laundry."

"They asked Mrs Edwards, that's Taffy's mother, what laundry we used," Jill said.

"So they went behind your backs. I've seen the new depositions, we know pretty well what they're going to say, but if we can find out exactly how they got the information it might be useful."

"How?" Hugh asked.

"I just don't know, Hugh. I feel it might be, that's all."

"I meant how are you going to do it?"

"A man at the *Banner,* named Crawley, used to know the boss of the Kwick-N-Clean. He's called Bostick." He looked at them interrogatively, but they shook their heads.

"I've never heard of him," Jill said.

"I've got an appointment to see him at half past five. Will you come, Hugh?"

"Of course."

"You're doing a lot for us. Don't think we're ungrateful," Jill said. She looked at her father. George Gardner had finished his pie, and was licking the crumbs off his finger.

Chapter Thirty-one

With the dexterity of a ballet dancer Hardy led them through the events of Guy Fawkes night. After the humdrum police and medical evidence, given by PC Buckley and the police surgeon, came Dr Mackintosh, who had been standing, as he said, some six yards from Corby at the time of the attack.

"Will you tell us exactly what you saw?"

"I've told you already about the firework throwing. Some of the boys rushed forward at Corby and grappled with him. I heard a voice say 'Get him, King,' and then a groan."

"You say some of the boys. How many?"

"I'm not sure. Two or three. You must realise that things were very confused. I just caught a glimpse of their faces."

"There was enough light for that?"

"Yes."

"Did you afterwards attend an identification parade?"

"I did."

"And pick out one of the boys you had seen?"

"That is correct."

"Will you tell us if that boy is in court."

"That one." The doctor pointed to Garney.

Gavin Edmonds devoted himself to establishing in cross-examination that the doctor might have recognised Garney from his photograph in the newspapers. Newton was brief but effective.

"You were unable to identify any other boy who attacked Corby?"

"That is so."

"And you are not certain whether two or three boys were involved in the scuffle?"

"I couldn't be sure. It was a dark night."

"To be sure, to be sure. And no moon."

"No. But there was the light from the bonfire."

"This light, however, wasn't enough to enable you to identify any boy except Garney?"

"No."

"And you were standing at just about this distance from Corby." Newton walked across the well of the court. He certainly looked very near to the doctor. Eustace Hardy got up, and looked distastefully down his long nose.

"My lord, the prosecution has never maintained that this witness was able to identify the prisoner Gardner. Is it necessary for my learned friend to indulge quite so obviously his sense of drama?"

Mr Justice Beckles looked over his spectacles. "This demonstration has some purpose, Mr Newton?"

"It has indeed, my lord. But this is my last question, if the witness may be allowed to answer it."

"Pray continue, Mr Newton."

"At about this distance?" Newton repeated. He struck no particular attitude but stood in the court, a dumpy, slightly ridiculous figure with his wig a little awry.

Dr Mackintosh looked uncertain. "I suppose so. These things seem rather different in daylight."

Newton looked at the jury, as though marking his position on their minds by means of a metaphorical chalk line. Then he went back to the bench and sat down.

Lopsided Joe Pickett, wearing his clothes like a tailor's dummy, looked an unpromising witness, but under gentle handling from Hardy he told a coherent tale. Here, as Hardy induced Pickett to tell the story, was a witness who had had a chance of looking closely at the boys when they were at the dance, who had been standing beside Corby and had seen two boys strike him, had seen a knife drawn, and had picked out both Garney and Gardner at the identification parade.

Gavin Edmonds made one dent in the identification, but it was a dent for which Hardy must have been prepared.

"You picked out the two prisoners at the identification parade," Edmonds said. "You're quite sure of that identification?"

"Certain sure."

"But you made some other identifications too, didn't you?"

"How's that?" Pickett's head went even more to one side.

"You identified some of the other boys," Edmonds said loudly, as though he were speaking to a slightly deaf imbecile. "Were they all the right boys? Were they, Mr Pickett?"

"Got two wrong," Pickett grumbled.

"So you identified four boys, and two of them were completely innocent people who had nothing at all to do with the case. That's so, isn't it? Isn't it, Mr Pickett?"

Pickett reluctantly admitted that apparently it was.

Magnus Newton stood up and teetered on his little legs. Subduing his melodious boom he said, "You were standing close to Corby that night, weren't you?"

"That's right."

"How close?" Newton asked invitingly. "Close enough to touch him?"

Pickett looked wary. "Ah. Wouldn't like to say I coulda touched him. No, don't think I coulda touched him."

"But closer than Dr Mackintosh?"

"Aye, closer than the doctor. Close enough to see," he said emphatically.

There was a hush as Newton walked slowly to that metaphorical chalk line he had made in the well of the court. "Would you say, supposing I was Corby, that you were about as near as this to me?"

"Could be. Or could be I was a foot or two farther away."

"A foot or two farther away. But still, you were nearer than Dr Mackintosh?"

"Aye, nearer than the doctor."

Newton thrust his head forward. His face was suddenly red and angry. "This is the distance at which Dr Mackintosh said he was standing. Were you nearer than this?" Pickett did not answer. Newton repeated the question.

"Mighta been a couple of feet nearer," Pickett said reluctantly.

"You *might* have been a couple of feet nearer than Dr Mackintosh. No more than that?"

"Suppose not."

"Dr Mackintosh was able to identify only one boy. I suggest that you could see no more than he did."

"Oh, I saw 'em all right."

"Do you regard yourself as so very much more observant than Dr Mackintosh?" Newton asked with heavy irony.

Joe Pickett's little eyes screwed up, a sideways grin spread over his face. "Not in the usual way, no. But Doctor wasn't wearing his glasses. Can't see too well without 'em."

There was a ripple, the merest ripple that quickly died, of something like laughter. Newton stared angrily at Joe Pickett for a moment, then walked slowly back to his place and went on asking questions. But the effect he was aiming at had been destroyed, and it was really almost unnecessary for Hardy to show in re-examination that whatever the precise spot on which Joe Pickett had been standing, he had certainly been nearer to Corby than had Dr Mackintosh, and that, while his identification of the two innocent boys had been a general one, his recognition of the two in the dock had been that they were positively attacking Corby. Newton's old trick had not come off, but perhaps he had planted a seed of doubt in some jurymen's minds.

Chapter Thirty-two

The Kwick-N-Clean laundry smelt of laundry, but from the office of the managing director, Mr Charles J Bostick, all laundry smell had been abolished. In fact almost all smell had been abolished from it, as though the mahogany-panelled green-carpeted room existed in a vacuum within the laundry – but a vacuum in which it was perfectly possible to live and breathe, and to look as fatly, heartily healthy as Mr Bostick, who now greeted them with a firm handshake, set them down in metal-legged semi-circular chairs that were a lighter shade of green than the carpet, and opened the cocktail cabinet. While he was pouring two pink gins and Hugh's plain Dubonnet, Mr Bostick talked.

"It's a long time since I heard from Edgar Crawley. We were up together, Edgar and I, and you could see that he was a brilliant fellow. I remember a little essay he wrote on – would it have been the Franco-Prussian War now – you gentlemen won't know, but I remember everybody said Edgar had a brilliant future ahead of him. And they were right. Mark you, it's no secret that Edgar always had a great eye for the main chance." He laughed uproariously.

"He hasn't lost it," Fairfield said.

Bostick laughed again. He was professionally genial, one of nature's Rotarians. "And so when I heard Edgar's voice on the telephone, I thought, there's only one reason why Edgar would want to talk to an old laundryman like me, he wants something out of me." He laughed so much at this that Hugh and Fairfield felt constrained to join him, in a modest way.

"And you were right," Fairfield said.

"I was right. That's Edgar." It seemed for a moment that Bostick would be set off again, but he controlled himself "Edgar said it was a matter of importance. That means it's something to do with the Guy Fawkes case. Am I right?"

"Right." Fairfield paused, then leaned forward. A little of the gin slopped on to his fingers. "Have you read about today's proceedings?"

"I'm a working man. I read the evening papers at home in an armchair."

"And nobody, no police official, has called to see you in relation to the case?"

"No. Why should they have done? I don't understand you." The geniality had vanished. Bostick was the kind of man, Hugh thought, who always expects to be cheated and cheats first to prevent it. He said sharply, "You're Bennett from the *Gazette*, right? I thought I'd seen you around."

"I'm sorry." Fairfield was covered with blurred apologetic confusion. "We're doing some unofficial detecting, Hugh and I."

"For the defence, of course. The *Banner's* backing this boy Gardner, I saw that. Good enough stunt, I suppose, though he's guilty as hell. What it's all got to do with me, that's what I don't understand. Don't like being brought into police business, except in the way of giving my sub for charities, taking a couple of tickets for a dance and so on."

"Part of the police case against Leslie Gardner is based on evidence connected with this laundry."

"Nothing said about it at the Magistrate's Court."

"No. This is additional evidence that has presumably been discovered since then," Fairfield said cautiously.

"What sort of evidence?"

"It's connected with the cleaning of a pair of grey trousers."

"At this laundry?"

"Yes."

"And you'd like to know how they got hold of it? So should I. Very much indeed."

"The Gardners use this laundry."

"Do they now? Well, I can tell you the police have made no inquiries of me." He pushed down a switch on his desk and spoke into a microphone. "Ask Miss Pligh to come up. At once, please. She's the manageress," he said, and then did not speak again but tapped with a pencil on his green leather desk until Miss Pligh, fat and friendly, came in.

"Ah, Miss Pligh." Bostick was almost a parody of the bonhomous democratic employer. "Just a small query you may be able to answer."

"Certainly."

"Have the police been in touch with you recently about any matter relating to the laundry?" He stared intently at her. Miss Pligh's not uncomely cheeks blushed a deep pink. "Have they?"

"I can explain."

"I shall be glad of that. Particularly why you thought fit not to tell me anything about it." Bostick did not look at anybody but the plump woman who wriggled slightly in front of him, but Hugh sensed that he was enjoying the presence of an audience.

"They said it was to be kept a secret."

"And who are 'they,' Miss Pligh?"

"The man from Scotland Yard. Sergeant Norman. I thought he'd get in touch with you himself."

"So you thought fit to keep the whole thing secret, did you?"

"I was worried, but I didn't like to say anything."

"Oh, really. I suppose that is what you call using your initiative?"

"I – "

"Do you? Is that what you call it? I can tell you what *I* call it. I call it downright disloyalty to the business that puts bread into your mouth. Shall I tell you the effect of what you have done? You have involved the Kwick-N-Clean in a sordid murder case. You have damaged our business, I don't know how much." Bostick had been almost shouting, fat hands gripping the desk. Now he leaned back. "I hope you are proud of yourself."

Miss Pligh burst into tears. Fairfield looked at the empty glass in his hand as though he disliked drink. "It may not be quite as bad as that. If Miss Pligh could tell us just exactly what happened."

"If that wouldn't be too much trouble. And if it doesn't mean breaking any promises made to Sergeant Norman," Bostick said with deadly sweetness.

Between sobs Miss Pligh told them the story. Bostick sat with arms folded.

"So Norman took the Gardners' laundry book," Fairfield said. "And he was excited about the date. Yes, I can see that."

"He didn't *take* the book, Miss Pligh kindly *gave* it to him," Bostick said. "Is there anything more you want to know? That's all? Then you can go, Miss Pligh. I'll talk to you later."

When she had gone, Bostick raised his hands above his head. "What can you do with them? Solid oak from the neck up. My word, old Edgar wouldn't put up with her for five minutes."

"She should have come to you. But I hope you won't – "

"Shan't get rid of her. They're all so stupid, I should get no one better. But she's not going to find life round here very easy for the next few weeks, I'll make sure of that." Bostick rubbed his hands together. The look on his face made Hugh feel sorry for Miss Pligh. He went to the cocktail cabinet. It was the first time Hugh had seen Frank Fairfield refuse a drink.

When they were out in the street he said, "What does Edgar Crawley do at the *Banner?*"

"He's the editor. But he's more than that. Also known as the direct pipeline to Lord Brackman."

"Is he anything like that man?"

"Edgar is seventeen different kinds of a horror. But no. He is nothing like Charles J Bostick."

In the unused front room at Peter Street, Van Gogh and Utrillo looked down on them. Jill sat frowning at the news and then asked, "What does it mean, exactly?"

"It means that the police think they've found proof positive that Leslie's tied up to the murder of Rocky Jones. The trousers came back on Friday afternoon. Do you remember taking them in?"

"I remember the laundry coming."

"And there was a pair of grey trousers in it?"

"I can't remember that. It's two months ago. There was nothing missing. I'd have to go by the book."

"The police have got the book. Didn't you realise it had been lost, and you'd been given a new one?"

"I suppose so. I didn't think about it. Why should I?"

For the first time, as he saw Fairfield grimly tugging away at this thread towards the nastiness at the end of it, a strand of lank hair falling over his rough forehead, the bloodshot eyes for once unblurred, Hugh realised consciously what made him a good crime reporter.

"We'll have to accept that the trousers did come back that afternoon. Leslie was picked up by the police straight from work in his old brown suit. He came back about midnight. He was picked up on Saturday morning straight from bed, and the trousers then had this mixture of sand and coal in the turn-ups. How did it get there if he wasn't wearing them late on Friday night?"

"Perhaps the laundry left it in?" Hugh suggested. "I don't think that horse will run. The laundry will say it's not possible that anything could have been left in after cleaning. And I think you'll find the police will be able to show the trousers have been worn."

"You believe he did it," Jill said suddenly. "You think he went out and killed Rocky Jones. Don't you?"

"What I believe doesn't matter. I'm telling you what the police think they have found out. That's the point we have to start from, Jill, you must understand that."

Jill put her head in her hands. Hugh found himself unable to discover his own beliefs. Leslie Gardner seemed to him a cipher, as are so many characters in criminal cases, and it was useless to ask whether this cipher was in reality the kind of youth who might have helped to kill a man and another boy. "Look at the facts," Lane was always saying. "Nothing else is important." But what conclusion could you reach when the facts of a story seemed confused beyond extrication? Desperately he said to Fairfield, "What *do* you believe?"

Like some great oracle, Fairfield answered, from his position under the Van Gogh self-portrait, the broad battered humanity of which he somehow, at a great distance, echoed. "I told you, it doesn't matter. What any of us believes doesn't matter. We play the game according to the rules. There's no other way to play it, no other way we can win."

"You still think we can win?" Jill asked.

"Of course we can win. First of all, Jill, I want you to tell me about Leslie's clothes, what they were, the sort of times he wore them, how often he had them cleaned, everything you can think of. Don't leave out anything, even if it seems silly."

"I'll try." There was a whistle from the kitchen. "That's the kettle. I'll make tea."

Hugh followed her. She turned and clung to him, kissed him passionately, then gripped his shoulders. "Hugh. This doesn't mean the end of it."

"If anybody can help us, Frank will." He was aware of evasiveness.

"Yes. Hugh, I'm so worried about Dad. He's changed. He missed a ward meeting last week, the first one for years."

He broached uneasily a delicate subject. "I suppose his teeth – "

"It was before he broke the plate. All he does is go to work, come home and eat and go to bed. He got off work this week, but he really doesn't seem much interested in the trial, I mean in what goes on. Tonight he had his supper and went straight to bed. Oh, Hugh, what have I done to him?"

"Are we going to get some tea?" Fairfield's head peered round the kitchen door. When they were back in the front room he said, patiently relentless, "What did Leslie usually wear when he went to the cottage?"

"How should I know? I didn't even know he went there."

"I mean when he went out and wasn't using his motor-bike, just said he was seeing the boys."

"Oh. Mostly his brown suit from work."

"How many pairs of grey trousers had he got?"

"Two. One made of worsted and the other gaberdine... "

It was after midnight when they left, and Hugh felt that they had discovered nothing. When he climbed the stairs to the flat Michael was sitting with his feet up, wrapped in a red and green striped dressing-gown. "How goes it, Romeo?"

"Oh, shut up."

"Was it Romeo tonight or the crime investigator's number one son? You haven't missed anything wildly exciting in court. There was one of those tremendously polite little interludes called brush between counsel, which look so furious when they're put on the stage, and are really so tame."

"I heard about it."

"I forgot, you get your news from the fountain-head. How is the fountain-head, by the way? Has the *Banner* propositioned you yet?"

"Not yet."

"And if they do, what will you say?"

"I don't know."

"I know what I'd say. I couldn't shake off the dust of this place fast enough. If you're offered the chance to get out, take it, and don't mind what anybody says." Michael had these moments of rare, surprising honesty. He dropped his book, a copy of Shaw's *Plays for Puritans,* to the floor, and looked vaguely reminiscent. "I met the most marvellous mare tonight. You know the local hospitals have a closed circuit radio programme? They asked me to do something about theatres in the city, and when I went up there was this red-head in the studio… "

Hugh made himself a cup of chocolate and listened for half an hour to Michael talking about the marvellous mare, before he went to bed.

Chapter Thirty-three

The tactics for treating child witnesses are pretty generally agreed. They must not be frightened or in any way coerced, or even pushed at all hard. If they turn inarticulate in the witness box it is usually better to let them stand down rather than try to squeeze from them a repetition of every word in their original statements. Any least hint of pressure, it is known, is liable to make a jury think that the counsel applying it is a potential mental torturer, a latter-day Mr Barrett. Eustace Hardy had these rules (which, naturally, apply only to respectable children and not at all to delinquents, who may be treated as roughly as you like) well in mind. His manner with children was perfect, that of a reasonably indulgent father who never descended to using the syrup of sentiment. It was said, no doubt with more than a touch of exaggeration, that Hardy always took a case which had a child witness in it because he knew that during examination or cross-examination of the child he could sway a jury temporarily, and sometimes even permanently, in his favour. So now Maureen Dyer, stiff in her best frock, relaxed gradually under the flow of easy questions asked in that silvery voice, and told quite readily of the man who had knocked her over, of the hard and sharp thing she had felt in his pocket, and of the knife shining in his hand.

"And then you went along to the identification parade," said father Hardy.

"Yes, and I picked out him." Maureen Dyer pointed to the slight figure of Leslie Gardner.

Her responses were becoming almost too ready. If he asked any more questions, Hardy decided, she might sound glib. He sat down.

Magnus Newton rose, puffing and smiling, an uncle with half a crown in his pocket which would be handed over if you gave the right answer.

"What were the fireworks you had on that Guy Fawkes night, Maureen?"

"Some yellow dragons and some fizz flares, and some sparklers."

"And when this man knocked into you, they all went on to the ground."

"Not the sparklers. I'd used them first. I don't like them as much as the others."

"Keep the best till last," Newton said with a laugh rather obviously artificial. It was apparent that, in dealing with children, he was not of Hardy's calibre. "And then your golden dragons were knocked to the ground."

"Yellow dragons, yes. But a nice man helped me to pick them up and light them, and they were all right."

"That's good," Newton said heartily. "Now, the thing that most interested you was your fireworks. So you didn't have much time to look at the man who knocked into you, did you?"

"Oh, but I saw him. I recognised him afterwards, didn't I?" She was wide-eyed.

"You're sure you weren't mistaken? You didn't have much time to look at him."

"Oh yes, I did see him. He was very close to me."

"Now, you say you felt something hard and sharp in his pocket. How could you tell that the thing was sharp."

"I just could, that's all."

"Did it come through the cloth and prick your hand?"

"Oh no. I just felt it, through the cloth, you know."

"But how could you feel something sharp through the cloth? It's hard to feel a sharp thing through a pocket, isn't it?"

"I don't know. I just did. And then I saw it afterwards. It was a knife."

Newton's tone was becoming with each question less that of the jovial uncle. The half-crown was on the verge of disappearance. "So you were knocked over. And when you got up you looked for your yellow dragons. Is that right?"

"Yes."

"Then when did you see the knife?"

"He drew it as he ran away from me. I saw it flash in the light."

Newton resisted the strong temptation to treat the girl as a delinquent. "You could only have seen that just as you got up. Don't you think you might have been mistaken?"

"Oh no."

All question of the half-crown gone, a cane almost audibly swishing in the background, so that his junior, Toby Bander, shifted uneasily, Newton said, "Then why didn't you say anything about the knife when you were first asked about all this?"

She hesitated, looked towards somebody, probably her father, said nothing. Newton repeated his question. Don't let her cry, he thought, don't let her cry.

Her under-lip quivered, but she didn't cry. "I suppose I just never thought of it."

"You didn't think of it," Newton said slowly, looking at the jury. He did not dare to ask any more questions. Hardy decided that there was a nail or two here which might usefully be driven home.

"When you were at the identification parade, Maureen, did you pick out the man at once?"

"Oh yes. There were a lot of others, but I knew this one."

"So there was no doubt in your mind?"

She shook her head vigorously. "Oh no."

"And are you just as sure about seeing the knife?"

"Yes. It was shining, you see."

Hardy nodded, smiled at her, and sat down. Mr Justice Beckles squeaked, "You may stand down, young lady. You may leave the box."

With the utmost self-possession, Maureen Dyer stepped out of the witness box and walked across to her father, who handed her an enormous teddy bear. Magnus Newton, who rarely used strong language, whispered to Toby Bander, "There goes a bloody little liar."

Chapter Thirty-four

The moments when he walked along the corridor into court, across the few feet to the witness box, muttered the conventional words, had for Hugh Bennett a dream-like quality of tension which was nevertheless unreal. It was as though he himself were on trial, or at least as though the whole ritual of the law was on this occasion specially and deliberately aimed at him. He found himself quite unable to look at the boys in the dock, in fear that – that what, precisely? That Leslie Gardner had assumed some stigmata that accused Hugh Bennett of responsibility for his present position? Absurd, of course, yet in the absurdity there was some element of truth.

"Your name is Hugh Bennett?"

"You are a reporter working with the *Gazette* newspaper in this city?"

"Yes."

"Will you tell the jury the reason for your presence at Far Wether that evening?"

Slowly he was led through an account of the evening, his conversation with Corby, his meeting with Maureen Dyer. All this was mere confirmation, which did not hold the attention of the court. Hardy went on.

"Will you tell us what you did after you saw the youth point at Corby?"

"He struck away my hand. Then I put my arms round him and felt something hard in his pocket. He pulled himself away from me and stumbled over the little girl. Then he ran towards Corby."

"You felt something hard in his pocket. Might that have been a knife?"

"I shouldn't like to say."

"But you must have an idea of what the object might have been. After all, you felt it in his pocket."

"Only for a moment. The whole of our contact was over in a few seconds." Thinking about it was like trying to decide with closed eyes the shape of an object in the mouth. "It was hard, and had hard edges. It might have been a cigarette case. I couldn't say it was a knife."

"Did you later attend an identification parade, and there pick out somebody as the man you had grappled with?"

"Yes."

"And is he in court now?"

"Yes." He pointed to Leslie Gardner, and then spoke the words that had given him so much anxiety. "But I am no longer sure of the identification."

There was silence in court. Hugh Bennett looked straight ahead of him. He had told nobody, not even Frank Fairfield, of the decision he had reached, believing that he should make up his mind alone, unaided.

There was a rustle just above him. The Judge peered down, eyes kind, words anti-climactic. "I am not sure if I heard that correctly."

"I am no longer sure of my identification," he said boldly. "I cannot identify Leslie Gardner as the person I struggled with on the green at Far Wether that night."

There was a sound in court at this answer, a sound like the expression of some great collective sigh.

Eustace Hardy's mind worked like a beautiful, logical machine, capable of working out with extraordinary speed a balance of probabilities. He had heard some sort of vague rumour that this young man had been associated with the *Banner,* the sensational paper that was putting up money for Gardner's defence. It would be possible for him to ask permission of the Judge, who was now looking at him inquiringly, to treat Bennett as a hostile witness and then to cross-examine him. But Bennett was not a witness of first importance, and he looked a determined young man. To treat him as a hostile witness might give the whole thing an importance it really didn't warrant. Better, then, to ask a few destructive questions and leave it at that. These were the thoughts that passed through Hardy's mind in the space of some thirty seconds. The decision he reached was moved partly, there can be no doubt, by a natural well-bred distaste for dramatic scenes in court. In the rich theatrical air that nurtured the great histrionic advocates of the first quarter of this century Eustace Hardy's talents would not have thrived.

There was nothing ironic in his silver voice as he said, "When did you make up your mind about this, Mr Bennett?"

"I've felt more and more doubtful in the past few weeks. I only made up my mind finally a couple of days ago."

"At the time of the identification parade you picked out Gardner immediately?"

"Yes."

"You had no hesitation at all."

"No."

"How do you explain that?"

Slowly he said, "I was present when Gardner was arrested, and caught a glimpse of him then. I had also met his sister. They look rather alike."

"So you think you may have been influenced by that?"

"I can't put that possibility out of my mind."

"And Miss Gardner is a friend of yours, perhaps?" This was a piece of nice guesswork, based on the way in which Hugh had mentioned her.

"Yes."

"Thank you. If Miss Gardner is in court I should like to ask her to stand up so that the jury may see how much she resembles her brother."

Jill stood up, came into the well of the court. She looked, Hugh thought, dismayingly little like her prison-pallid brother. Eustace Hardy nodded and sat down, feeling that he had dealt adequately with an awkward but unimportant issue. This, however, was not at all the opinion of his junior, A V Carter, who thought, and even in private company afterwards said, that the old man had made a bad mistake in not tearing young Bennett to pieces.

The way was now clear for Newton to destroy the effect of Maureen Dyer's testimony, and he did so with relish. He established that Hugh had not seen a knife flashing, or any sign of one, and that in Hugh's opinion it was not possible to have seen Gardner for long enough to identify him with certainty. It was undoubtedly a morning for the defence, although, as Newton said sagely to Toby Bander at lunchtime, you never can tell what a jury will think.

Hugh saw Jill and her father just outside the court. "I want to say thank you," she said.

He would have liked to explain the complication of the whole thing, to express all the fine shades of it, to say that her face had so truly overlaid her brother's in his mind that he was utterly unsure of himself and so would have liked to enter not the positive denial that had come out in court but a statement saying that he was not a competent witness in the matter. But of course none of this came out.

"It was a brave thing to do, wasn't it, Dad?"

"I'm sorry you had to stand up like that."

Mr Gardner, sunken-faced and greyish, said, "I never doubted Hugh would do the right thing, never doubted it."

"We're going to have lunch. But perhaps you'd better not come with us." She pressed his hand as they parted, and in her glance there was something uncomfortably conspiratorial.

Chapter Thirty-five

When Fairfield had telephoned through his story he went back to the bar of the Goat, where Michael Baker sat with a glass of beer and a ham sandwich in front of him. Fairfield lifted his pink gin with trembling hand, drank it in two gulps, and ordered another.

"Your boy did well by his side this morning," Michael said.

"He's not my boy."

"Oh, come on. Don't tell me you didn't know. You've been chasing up the clues together."

The eyes behind the great spectacles considered Michael incuriously. "I didn't know."

"I didn't know either, and I share a flat with him, so that makes two of us," Michael said with his agreeable smile. "Our Hugh's really flying independent colours, isn't he?"

"Our Hugh," Fairfield said solemnly, "is nobody's boy but his own."

At just about the same time Edgar Crawley was saying much the same thing, in rather different words, at lunch in Lord Brackman's flat. A picture window extended the whole thirty-foot length of the dining-room, and Brack and Crawley sat on black metal chairs at a white marble dining-table. The chair legs were thin and long and they looked rather small on the chairs, rather like two aged children, but the *Banner* readers on whom they looked out were, from this vantage point eight floors up, even smaller. Lord Brackman was eating his usual lunch, a slice of cold beef with a salad of grated raw vegetables and Ryvita. He drank soda water. Crawley ate a large steak and drank half a bottle of a good claret.

"Interesting, very interesting," Brack said. The important points in Fairfield's story had been telephoned through to the flat at once. "This boy Bennett. What about him?" Brack's voice was lighter, and less whiningly irritable, than it sounded on the telephone. He had a small head with features rather squashily irresolute, redeemed by a sweep of beautiful silky grey hair. The body below it was short and fat, the little legs dangling from the spindly chair hardly reached the floor.

"The reporter on the *Gazette*? He's been helping Fairfield."

"Yes. What's he like?"

Crawley knew that a literal answer to the effect that he did not know would be unacceptable. It was his business (that was the unspoken implication) to know such things, by intelligence or intuition, to express an opinion upon which Brack would form *his* opinion, of dissent or agreement. All this Crawley knew and acknowledged, and it was without a flicker of hesitation that he said, "To me he sounds interesting."

"Fairfield's influenced him?"

"No. We had no idea this was coming." Crawley took a sip of claret. "I should say he made up his own mind. Absolutely."

"It was a good idea of mine, this. Worked out well." To this statement Crawley felt it unnecessary to make reply. "I like independence." Independent spirits both, they looked down upon the figures below, every one of them lacking free will. "This boy might be good. I think we could use him." Brack suddenly got off his chair, flung down his napkin, walked to one end of the room and bounced down upon a metal-framed bed-chair covered with bright interwoven

174

plastic strips. He tilted the bed-chair so that he could look out of the window, produced a toothpick and began energetically to dig fragments of food from his teeth. "Wasting his time in the provinces. When this thing is over, get him up." Staring intently out of the window, not for a moment looking at Crawley, Brack said sharply, "That city fire story. Why did it miss the early editions? The *Mail* had it, and the *Express.*"

It was obvious to Crawley that he would not be allowed to finish the steak or the claret. He got up, moved to a chair beside Brack, and began to explain. It seemed that the news editor was not quite measuring up to his job.

Chapter Thirty-six

The most important parts of a criminal trial are often the least dramatic. So it was in the Guy Fawkes case. During the afternoon of the trial's second day Charkoff, Taffy Edwards and Ernie Bogan went into the box and told their stories of the joke that had turned suddenly, and as they said against their expectation, to crime. Patiently Hardy constructed the picture, the boys setting out on their motorcycles, pockets stuffed with fireworks, subtly he conveyed to the jury the idea that these boys were of less than normal intelligence, tools in the hands of their acknowledged leader, King Garney, and his trusted lieutenant, Leslie Gardner. He did not try to arouse any sort of sympathy for them, but contented himself with showing that these were boys who would never initiate violence. Charkoff and Edwards admitted carrying knives, which they had thrown away after leaving Far Wether, on the way back to the city. They had done so at King's order. King and Leslie Gardner had thrown away their knives too. They had all dropped them into the Farlow river, which ran near to the road. The three boys did not positively say that they had seen Garney or Gardner attack Corby, but they recounted damning fragments of conversation.

"When you stopped to dispose of these knives in the river, was anything said about what happened?" Hardy asked Taffy Edwards.

"Yes. King says to me, 'You keep your mouth shut about this, Taffy. We haven't been there.' And I said I wouldn't talk, but I asked what had happened, see, because I just didn't know. And King says, 'We did him. We did that bastard.'"

"What did you understand him to mean by that?"

"Why, that they'd done Corby."

"Attacked him?"

"That's right."

"And who did you understand him to mean by 'we'?"

"Himself and Les."

"That is, Leslie Gardner. Now, when you got back you parted, didn't you?"

"That's right."

"Did you arrange to meet again?"

"Yes, at the Rotor."

"That is, the Rotor Dance Hall?"

"That's right. And Rocky Jones, he says he doesn't like it, doesn't think he'll come along, and King says to him, 'You'll come if you know what's good for you. We stick together. The Peter Street lot's got no use for squealers.'"

"Did Gardner say anything?"

"Yes. He said, 'Do as King says, Rocky, or you'll be in trouble.'"

"Was anything further said about what had happened at Far Wether?"

"Rocky asks what really happened, he isn't sure, and King says, 'We gave him the knife,' and then says he shouldn't be surprised if he croaked, and bad luck to him anyway."

By the time that these boys had given their evidence, and it had been supplemented by Jean Willard from the Rotor, the case against Garney seemed overwhelming. Gavin Edmonds did his best to whittle down what they said, but although it was easy enough to show the boys as contemptible, it was less easy to dispute the probability of what they were saying. Unimpeachably honest witnesses had already given their opinion that Corby had been attacked by two boys, and now here were three of them implicitly identifying the other two, and doing so not simply in their statements to the police, which Edmonds suggested had been obtained by a mixture of coercion and bribery, but telling Jean Willard very much the same story in the Rotor on the night of the crime. Edmonds made what he could of the fact that Jean Willard was a discarded girlfriend of Garney's, he was ironical and indignant in turn, but the evidence against Garney piled up and up while the boy stood gripping the sides of the dock with his big dark hands.

Magnus Newton's task in relation to these witnesses was less difficult, for there was, after all, little in what the boys said that directly involved Gardner.

"When Garney made his remark that 'We did that bastard,' he did not mention Leslie Gardner by name," he said to Edwards.

"No. But they were always around together."

"The fact is," Newton said in an agreeable, confidential tone, "you've really got no basis at all for thinking that Gardner attacked Corby, have you?"

Edwards stared at him with his mouth open, then looked at the Judge for help. Mr Justice Beckles said gently, "If you could perhaps rephrase the question, Mr Newton."

Newton rocked on his heels, then said loudly, "Did you see Gardner attack Corby?"

"No."

"Did Garney say that Gardner had attacked Corby?"

"No, he didn't, not by name."

"He didn't mention Gardner's name at all?"

"No."

Newton looked at the jury, decided that they had taken it in, and passed on. If they had not understood the point on this occasion they certainly did so when Newton repeated exactly the same form of questioning to Charkoff and Bogan.

What he accomplished, or at least what he intended, was to separate Garney from Gardner in the jury's mind.

If Newton was modestly pleased with his success in this respect, however, Hardy was not alarmed. The case against Gardner in relation to the death of Corby lacked something of the real solidity which finally convinced a jury. But there was still the damning evidence of the grey trousers, the evidence that was proof conclusive of Gardner's guilt. The first shot of this vital encounter was fired when, late that afternoon, Hardy's scientific witness briskly gave evidence, first of the bloodstains found on the boys' jackets, and then of the mixture of sand and coal dust found in Gardner's trouser turn-ups.

"Did you make a note about the condition of these trousers in your report?" Hardy asked.

"Yes. I said that these were very nice, smart trousers, nicely pressed, and by the look of them newly cleaned."

"They had been worn since cleaning, however?"

"Oh yes, they had been worn. But very little."

Hardy sat down with a satisfied nod. Newton got up and stood puffing and swaying on his feet for so long that the Judge squeaked at last, "Mr Newton?"

"Yes, m'lord. Now, Mr – " Newton looked down at his notes, elaborately forgetful – "Mr – ah – Price, let us deal first with the matter of what you call the significant bloodstains on Gardner's jacket. This is a technical term, is it not, this word significant?"

"I don't think so. It means that the stains are not absolutely microscopic. They can be seen with the naked eye."

"Ha. I am obliged. But it *doesn't* necessarily mean, does it, that these stains, however and whenever they were made, have any significance at all in this case?"

"That is hardly for me to say."

"These were stains of Gardner's own blood group, were they not?"

"They were."

"So that he may perfectly well have cut himself at some time or other, and got blood on his jacket?"

"Not 'at some time or other.' These stains were recent when I examined the jacket."

"How recent? Could you fix a date to them?"

"No, that is impossible."

"And they may perfectly well be Gardner's own blood so far as you, as a scientific expert, can tell?"

"They may be, yes."

"I am obliged. Now, Mr Price, I should like to turn to the trousers. The implication here is that Leslie Gardner wore these trousers on the evening of 6th November, when Jones was killed. Does your scientific skill enable you to say – ah – on exactly what day this mixture of sand and coal dust got into the turn-ups?"

"No, sir. It does not."

"It might as well have been on 6th October as on 6th November, as far as you are concerned?"

"Yes."

"And this view of yours about the trousers being newly cleaned, and having been worn since cleaning, was that based on your expert scientific knowledge?"

"No. Just on my powers of observation," Price replied smartly.

"I am obliged. Now, Mr Price, if you came home after midnight one night, after having been grilled – I believe that is the significant phrase – for several hours by the police, and then went out again with the intention of killing somebody, would you put on a pair of newly cleaned and pressed grey trousers?"

Price smiled faintly, and lifted his shoulders in a shrug. Mr Justice Beckles looked reprovingly at Newton and seemed about to make some caustic observation, when Newton abruptly sat down.

He left Eustace Hardy wondering just what counsel for the defence could be playing at. Hardy was not, however, a man who fought his cases with deep passion, or who allowed himself to be perturbed by the eccentricities of counsel opposed to him. A legal classicist, Hardy had an unlikely taste for a romantic treatment of history, and he read himself to sleep that night with the third volume of Macaulay's *History of England.*

Twicker, however, was disturbed. He held a conference at six-thirty with Norman, Langton and the Chief Constable. They decided that the evidence against Gardner was watertight, or as watertight as they could make it, and that Newton was simply adopting the last refuge of a counsel in distress, facetious irrelevance. Twicker remained slightly unconvinced by his own arguments. He slept little that night.

Norman slept soundly. He dreamed of naked women jumping through a hedge.

Hugh Bennett did not find the emotional release he had expected from admitting in evidence his inability to identify Gardner. The encounter with Jill should perhaps have prepared him for his reception in the office, but he was in fact taken quite unaware when Lane, puffing bluely from one of his cigars, said, "So you've done it. When does the train leave?"

"What's that?"

"I hear they're putting on a Bennett Special Express," the news editor said. "For young reporters on their way up. To London, I mean."

Hugh understood then. He sat down beside his typewriter, pulled out a notebook, and began furiously to type a paragraph for the gossip column.

"One more boy from the backwoods smells the sweet smell of success," Lane said. "But we'll say no more about it, shall we, Hugh? Just put a penny in old Lane's hat when you see him begging in the streets next Christmas, that's all I ask."

Half an hour later Clare came in and put a copy of the *Evening Standard* under his nose. "You've made the front page."

Hugh read the headlines: GUY FAWKES WITNESS SENSATION. LOCAL REPORTER RETRACTS EVIDENCE. He nodded, and folded over the paper. Clare sat on the desk beside him, her long legs swinging.

"He must be persuasive, your friend Fairfield. What did they promise you, Hugh, a job as understudy? It's just a matter of waiting till he gets d.t.s, is that what they said?"

"Fairfield knew nothing about it."

"You're a bit of a dark horse. I'd like to get to London as much as anybody, but there are some things I wouldn't do."

Lane leered at her, yellow-fanged. "Would you sell your beautiful body, girlie?"

"Oh, you. But I mean it." Clare got off the desk, stuck her nose in the air. "Some things are really a bit much."

Hugh walked out of the room and slammed the door. In the corridor he met Grayling. "In the news again, I see," the editor said without smiling. "You really can't seem to keep out of it, can you?"

"I was called to give evidence."

"That was a painful necessity. But to say first of all that you identified somebody and then that you didn't, that's, eh, a little sensational."

"It's the truth."

"I'll tell you just what the chairman said about it when I spoke with him on the telephone. He said, 'Eh, Grayling,' he said, 'this kind of thing shows, eh, a disturbing lack of responsibility.' I felt bound to agree with him."

"You mean if I made a mistake I should have stuck to it."

"I'll say no more, Bennett. I'll say no more."

The door of Farmer Roger's little room was open. Within, a grey head could be glimpsed, brooding over copy. Hugh hesitated, fatally. The head was raised.

"Ah, Hugh, my boy, come in. You see a literary artist in the final throes. Polish, polish, polish, it's the first rule of style. Was it Stevenson who said that? And how many of our readers appreciate it, I ask you? How many care whether a piece is written well or badly? We do it to please ourselves, Hugh, that's the way of it, to satisfy the mysterious something, the force that drives us on to produce the best we can, and not to be satisfied with anything else. You know the old phrase, virtue is its own reward, it has no others. And what is it I'm hearing about you, my boy, what's the news that's cried in the marketplace? Don't go away, I must speak to you seriously."

How can it be, Hugh wondered, although he did not put it to himself in quite those terms, that a man can appear in one light a profound philosopher and in another a sententious old bore? He tried deliberately to plug his ears against the tide of words that flowed over him, but was unable to avoid hearing phrases.

"...the glittering prize that always eludes us...was it Chesterton who said that the glitter is the gold?...watched over you like a son...exercise of Christian charity...the great law of life...a bad influence, a true limb of Satan...to use a homely simile, fouling your own nest...was it Huxley, not always a favourite of mine but at times a wise and wonderful man, who talked about the bitch goddess Success?"

"Shut up, you canting old hypocrite." Hugh shouted, as he had never thought that he could or would shout, at Farmer Roger. "I changed my evidence because I wasn't sure. Hasn't one of you got the decency to believe that?"

That evening he got drunk for the first time in his life. He took drink for drink with Frank Fairfield in the American Bar of the Grand, and then in half a dozen pubs. He remembered little of the evening, except that he said over and over again to Fairfield, "You know the truth, Frank, you didn't know what I was going to say when I went in the box. That's the truth, isn't it?"

"That's the truth. You made up your own mind."

He thumped the bar counter. "Why won't any of them believe it?"

Fairfield said consideringly, "I think Michael does."

"Good old Michael. But why doesn't Jill? If you'd seen the way she looked at me afterwards."

He repeated variations on the same theme, no doubt with infinite tedium, for the rest of the evening. Fairfield said very little, but remained wrapped behind his curtain of drink. In a sense, Hugh thought afterwards, nothing could have been kinder than this courteous silence. Before the pubs closed Hugh became very drunk, and Fairfield took him back to the flat in a taxi. The stairs seemed to Hugh to have the consistency of jelly. At the top of them Michael was standing.

"Ah, the disappearing witness. Your girl's been here for you. She left a note. My word, you're drunk."

"Where's the note?" The words moved unsteadily in front of him, but there were not many of them. *"Hugh. I think I said something wrong today. Just the way you looked. Sorry. You were wonderful. I don't understand much. I told you, just a meat and two veg girl. Love, Jill."*

When Hugh had managed to read this he flopped back in the arm-chair, laughing helplessly. Fairfield and Michael put him to bed.

Chapter Thirty-seven

On the following morning Hardy unrolled his wares publicly for the first time, as it were, displaying the trail of evidence that had not been made public. First Twicker, erect, gauntly anxious, to tell of the visit to Platt's Flats, and of the sample of sand and coal dust taken from outside the back door, and to say that the sample had proved identical with that taken from Gardner's turn-ups. Then Norman, big and cocky, to tell of his inquiries at the Kwick-N-Clean laundry.

"Do you produce in court now the laundry book handed to you by the manageress, Miss Pligh?" Hardy asked.

"I do."

"And does this book show that a pair of grey trousers was returned cleaned to the Gardners on Friday, November the sixth?"

"It does."

"Have you examined the book for any other entries relating to the cleaning of grey trousers?"

" I have, sir."

"And what did you find?"

"The only other entry related to a pair of trousers cleaned in June."

To tie the last knots, there was the van driver, who testified that he had delivered the laundry on that Friday afternoon, and that it had been taken in by Miss Gardner.

The grey trousers had been, as usual, in a separate brown paper bag.

"I don't see how Newton's going to touch this evidence," Hardy had said to his junior earlier in the morning. "It's a beautifully neat consecutive chain, perfectly logical and clear."

"How would you handle it if you were Newton?"

Hardy's face was alight with intellectual pleasure. This kind of problem was one that he found extremely congenial. "I think, you know, I think I should be inclined to ask as few questions as possible. Play it down all the time, pick a few small holes perhaps, and then later on try to convince the jury that the whole thing isn't very important." Hardy's features took on that look of disdainful superiority which helped to explain why he had few friends. "But I doubt if Newton will see it in quite the same light."

Apparently, however, Newton did see it in the same, or a very similar, light. He asked no questions at all of Twicker or the van driver, and his interrogation of Norman was mild, and almost vague.

"How did you discover that the Gardner family used the Kwick-N-Clean laundry?"

"I made inquiries in the neighbourhood."

"From the family?"

"Not from the family," Norman said stolidly.

"Wouldn't it have been easier to ask the family what laundry they used and where things were cleaned, and so on?" Newton flapped his hand to indicate that this was a generality.

"I thought it better in this instance, sir, to make inquiries elsewhere."

"I see. And then at the laundry itself did you speak to the managing director, Mr – ah – Mr Bostick?

"No, sir. Simply to Miss Pligh."

"And that was for the same reason, to keep the inquiry quiet?"

"I wanted to confine it to as few people as possible, yes."

"Was that so that the defence shouldn't get to know of it too soon?" Newton asked mildly.

Hardy was on his feet. "I am advised that the defence knew of this evidence in good time before the opening of the trial, my lord."

Mr Justice Beckles peered, squeaked. "Are you suggesting that this was not so, Mr Newton?"

Newton waved again, airily. "I withdraw the observation, my lord."

"In that case it was a most improper question." Mr Justice Beckles was squeakily indignant.

"Should I be right in saying that this was the extent of your inquiry regarding the grey trousers, that once you had discovered that they had been returned to Miss Gardner on November the sixth, you asked no further questions about them?" Newton asked Norman.

"That is right."

Hardy re-examined briefly, to establish even more firmly in the jury's minds the fact that the trousers could not possibly have been worn before the evening of November the sixth. Then he said: "That is the case for the Crown, my lord."

Mr Justice Beckles nodded, looked at the clock. "This will be a convenient time at which to adjourn for lunch."

Chapter Thirty-eight

The evidence had been interesting enough in its way, but still the journalists had been disappointed of their morning fireworks. There had been none of the cuts and thrusts, the almost downright accusations of lying, that make good copy. Some of the crime reporters decided that Newton was resigned to letting nature take its course, others believed that some stupendous card remained still up his sleeve, and one or two of these latter tried – although they should have known better – to get some information out of the *Banner's* crime reporter. But Fairfield, sitting on the bar stool that was now regarded in the Goat as almost his personal property, ate his ham sandwiches and drank his bitter and refused to be drawn, even by Michael.

"You know, this is awfully like the trial of Mary Duggan or an Agatha Christie play or something," Michael said. "Some really smashing actress – like Nita Elvin, who was at the Theatre Royal last week – is going to give evidence and cry, 'The boy is innocent, he spent the night with me.' Right?"

"Wrong."

"I thought so. You do know what's going to happen though, don't you?"

"A bit of it, yes."

"I don't see how you can get round the trousers. Back from laundry Friday afternoon, found on Saturday full of

188

muck out of Platt's Flats. What's the answer? I simply can't wait to find out."

Michael did wait, however, waited through an opening speech by Gavin Edmonds, in which he said that there was nothing beyond vague suspicion to link Garney with either crime, and to a speech by Magnus Newton, stressing the same thing, and emphasising that the defence would call a witness who would say that on the night of November the fifth it was too dark to distinguish one face from another. Michael thought that Newton was going to avoid any reference to the trousers. but he came to them almost at the end.

"One of the points that the prosecution has made a great deal of, ladies and gentlemen, is related to a pair of trousers belonging to Leslie Gardner, a pair of trousers sent to the Kwick-N-Clean laundry for cleaning, and returned by them on November the sixth. I might fairly say, I think, that in the welter of fancies and improbabilities that make up the prosecution case against my client, this is put forward as the one solid fact that holds all the rest together. It is said that these same trousers were found on the following day to have traces of coal and sand in the turn-ups, that this mixture could only have come from Platt's Flats, and that this positively proved Gardner's presence there on that Friday night. You may have noticed, ladies and gentlemen, that I did not spend much time in cross-examination relating to this matter. That is because Gardner has a complete answer to it. He will go into the box, and you will hear from him that these trousers were never sent to the Kwick-N-Clean laundry, and hence never came back from that laundry, that they were another pair of trousers altogether... "

The reporters began to write with frantic eagerness. The secret was about to be revealed, then? But Newton said no more, and their curiosity remained unappeased, for now

Garney entered the witness box. And this, the reporters knew, was a lost one, for this one there was in practical terms no hope. There are racing outsiders that come triumphant home, and zero will sometimes fortify optimists on a roulette wheel, but for Garney the only chance lay in the possibility that somebody on the jury, one could almost go further and say some woman on the jury, would be romantically impressed by his youth and dark handsomeness, and would hold out staunchly for acquittal. It was necessary only to look at the three housewives who sat in the jury box, embattled images of respectability, two of them lean and hard-fleshed as though their bodies had been cut from wood, and the fat third one tougher still, the bulbous curves of her cheek and nose like solid rock, to realise that King Garney's chances were small indeed. It seemed that he understood this himself for he wore in the witness box the manner of spitting defiance that some great animal may have when finally boxed. From such useless violence the human animal is in general mercifully free. We feel it natural for human beings at times of their own impending utter destruction to collapse and cry, and Garney seemed to some of those who watched him snarling and snapping at his own counsel, Gavin Edmonds, something less, and yes, perhaps something more than human.

"He's wonderful," Michael Baker whispered to Fairfield. "Don't you think he's wonderful?" In reply Fairfield's lips shaped the words, *Look at the other.* Michael looked and saw Leslie Gardner leaning forward, lips parted, staring across the court at the figure in the witness box with all the intensity of a lover. Yet, although Gardner was immature, there was nothing feminine about him. It was, rather, as if the boy in the dock heard the boy in the witness box speaking for some outcast group of the inarticulate, as if in

190

all these long proceedings that had been given their deliberate weight and pomp through centuries of precedent and subtle change and in all these arguments conducted by the finest and fairest kind of legal logic, this animal defiance of Garney's was for Leslie Gardner the only thing that made sense. Garney, as he stood there in the box, offering answers that were often transparent lies, trying with the lowest sort of cunning to turn each incident to his own benefit, seemed to the perhaps over-impressionable Michael Baker to be asserting rights that did not belong at all to this court or to legal processes, the right to behave as he wished, the right to come roaring into Far Wether on a motorcycle and kill quite casually the man against whom he bore a grudge, the right to destroy a traitor to his self-constructed code. It was not that Garney admitted doing any of these things in his evidence, but that in his attitude there rested the implication that whether or not he had done them was of no importance.

This might be wonderful, as Michael Baker had incautiously whispered, but it was not law. In that time and place Garney had no weapons at all against the silver tongue that wounded him again and again in the long passage of Eustace Hardy's cross-examination. Recollection of all this was blurred by what happened afterwards, but at the time everybody – that is, the reporters, and the literary gentlemen who like to attend criminal cases, and the solicitors, and, a little reluctantly perhaps, the barristers – were agreed that this was one of the classic cross-examinations, and that whatever remnant of a chance Garney might have had before Hardy rose had disappeared completely by the time that the prosecuting counsel sat down. If there was one thing that mitigated the triumph it was that the struggle was so unequal, that Garney seemed not merely to lack the weapons but also the wish to defend himself. And although guilt by association has no legal existence, there was no doubt in anybody's mind that the effect produced by Garney in the witness box must have prejudiced Leslie Gardner's chance of acquittal.

Chapter Thirty-nine

Hugh nursed his hangover until midday and then, strengthened by several cups of tea, went into the office. He spent the afternoon interviewing a number of people, including the city architect and surveyor, the chairman of the city council, some local residents and small shopkeepers, to ask their opinions about the construction of a vast car park on an area of waste ground near the city centre. He found, not surprisingly, that the shopkeepers were in favour of the project, the local residents considered it an outrage, and the city authorities regarded it as a painful necessity. It was quite an interesting job, but his head ached, and he did not do it well. He walked back to the flat leaning against an east wind that seemed to cut through his thin raincoat. Snow that never fell hung like a permanent threat in the grey sky. He felt himself to be shivering, and was lying on the bed when the doorbell rang. He went down the stairs past the cabbage smell, and let in Jill.

"You weren't in court today," she said almost severely, as she took off her coat and stood warming her hands by the electric fire.

"I was ill. Not ill. Last night I got drunk."

"Drunk," she said indignantly. "Whatever for?"

"Giving evidence got me down, I suppose. And then going to the office afterwards got me down too. Thank you for the note."

"Oh, I see. That's all right. I'm sorry I was so – "

"What?"

"Nothing."

"I've been out on a job. How did it go today?"

"It was that hateful Garney. He's been the trouble with Leslie all along. Leslie's a good boy."

"You mean he tried to involve Leslie when he gave evidence?"

"Oh no. It's just the way he goes on, Garney, I mean, and the way he looks, as though he doesn't care about anything. I hate him. Hardy just tore him to pieces, and now everyone says how bad it is for Leslie. Why are you shivering?"

"I'm cold."

"Go and lie down. I'll make a hot drink." He put on pyjamas and got into bed, still shivering. She went on talking from the kitchenette. "I don't know what's happened to Dad, he's so queer. Do you think it's just breaking his plate that's upset him?"

"Perhaps. When will it be done?"

"About ten days, they say. But the whole thing seems to have changed him. We shall have to leave."

"What?"

"I said we shall have to leave. All of us. We can't stay here." She appeared at the door, steaming cup in hand. "As soon as Leslie's out we must go."

"Yes."

Her lips were trembling. She no longer looked pretty. "You think he did it, don't you? You think they'll find him guilty."

"No."

"You do. Oh, Hugh, I'm so miserable." She put the cup down carefully on the chipped brown chest of drawers and flung herself beside him on the bed. Her lips as they met his were warm and yielding, she answered his embraces not with passion exactly but with a desperate need for solace, so that she could not be quick enough to unzip her dress and get into bed with him. Afterwards they did not talk much. She cried a little, and he sipped the drink, which was no longer hot. But by this time he had stopped shivering.

Chapter Forty

Leslie Gardner took the witness stand on the following morning. His slightness, and his immature good looks, gave an impression of extreme youth that was in his favour, but that carried also the unfortunate implication that he might easily be persuaded to follow a boy of stronger will than his own. It would be part of Newton's job to exploit Gardner's youth and innocence, yet to eradicate any feeling that he was one of nature's cat's paws. Gardner's manner did not help him. He wore his narrow-shouldered suit and his bright strip of tie in a way that was almost a parody of Garney's, and every so often his fingers would go up to the knot of this tie and self-consciously straighten it. At first so nearly inarticulate that he was asked by the Judge to speak up, he gathered self-confidence and became objectionably pert in his answers. For much of this Newton had been prepared. The boy must be given time to settle down, and his own early questions were intentionally bumbling and slow.

"On this night, Guy Fawkes night, then, you bought fireworks and went out to Far Wether?"

"Yes."

"What did you mean to do out there?"

"We were going to give this chap, Corby, a bit of a scare. Let the fireworks off at him, like."

Newton puffed anxiously, leaned forward. "Tell me this. Was there any thought of making a violent attack on Corby in your mind?"

Fingers to tie. "Course not."

"You are quite sure that nothing of the sort was ever mentioned?"

"Quite sure."

"Did you have a knife in your pocket?"

"Yes." Gardner said it reluctantly. He had admitted this only after considerable pressure at another prison interview. Newton felt sure that in this case an admission of everything that seemed probable would strengthen his hand in relation to the two or three points of real importance.

"Where did you carry it?"

"In my hip pocket."

"Were you intending to use this knife?"

The court was still. Gardner seemed almost visibly to compose himself to seriousness. "No, sir."

"Then why did you carry it?"

"It was a sort of a badge. We all carried them."

"You all carried them. You are sure of that?"

"We all carried them sometime or other."

"Can you be sure that you were all carrying them that night?

"No. I mean to say, we didn't show them, or anything like that. We just carried them for fun."

"Was it a knife like this one?" Newton produced a thin sheath, pressed a button, and a blade flicked out. Gardner nodded. Newton was about to continue his examination when the Judge spoke.

"Ah – just a moment, Mr Newton. Do I understand you to say that these knives were simply a kind of badge, and that you never used them?"

Gardner was obviously uneasy at this intervention. "That's right."

"And you are saying that you never used the blade of your knife? Never used it at all."

"Oh well, I don't know. Cut wood and that." This was a mutter.

"What did you say?"

"Said I might have used it to cut wood, carve my name or something."

"And did you do so?"

Gardner looked both baffled and frightened. "Do what?"

Mr Justice Beckles looked at the jury. His voice achieved a notable squeak, but he hastily brought it back into range. "You originally said that you never used the knife. If that is literally true, you never used the blade at all. If what you mean is that you used it only very occasionally, you would be likely to remember carving wood or doing other things with it. Do you understand?" Gardner nodded, staring in a mesmerised way at the Judge. "I am now going to ask – remember that you are upon your oath – whether you ever threatened any other person with it?"

Gardner was shaking his head almost before the Judge had finished. "No. Oh no. I never did that."

"Did you ever see any of your friends use their knives to threaten anybody?"

"No. Never."

"I want to be quite clear about this. What you are telling us is that you all had these knives but that, to the best of your knowledge, none of you ever used them to threaten anybody at all."

"That's right." Gardner touched his tie and repeated hopefully, "It was sort of a badge."

The Judge, his brief flare of energy gone, sank back. Newton got up again, writhing inwardly. You had only to look at the jury to see what they thought of the replies. Why did the boy have to be such a fool? But the boy must not be frightened. With his rich, melodious croak subdued to

198

gentleness he said, "Now then, I want you to tell the jury in your own words exactly what happened when you got to Far Wether."

"We cut off our engines after putting the spots on first to make sure this was the right show. Then we went across the grass. King – that's Garney – was in front, I think, but it was pretty dark and you couldn't see much. Somebody said, 'Let him have it' and I could see Corby standing near the fire and I threw my fireworks."

"Who said 'Let him have it'?"

"I don't know. There was too much noise, with the fireworks and everything."

"And where were you standing at this time?"

"Sort of in the middle, we'd all spread out, see. Then I heard a lot of shouting going on, and there was a kind of a cry, and someone shouted 'Let's go' and we ran for our bikes and went."

This in effect was Gardner's whole story of his actions out at Far Wether. He had not pushed over Maureen Dyer, he had not tangled with Hugh Bennett, he had not shouted "Get him, King," and, although he agreed with the boys who had turned Queen's Evidence about King's remark on the way home that "We did that bastard," he insisted that King had never referred to him, and had not meant to do so. As Newton, a ponderous spider, spun his verbal web, as Gardner gathered strength and fluency of expression, it could be seen that Leslie Gardner was no more linked than any of Garney's other satellites to the death of Corby. What was there against him beyond a few dubious identifications made in the light of a bonfire? So, with the ground laid at careful length, Newton came to the following day.

"On leaving your work that day, Friday, what happened?"

"The police met us outside the gates and took us down to the station."

"Did they tell you the reason?"

"Not then, no. At the station they did. But we guessed it already."

"You guessed that it was to do with the attack on Corby?"

"Yes."

"How long were you at the station?"

"It was just after twelve o'clock when they let us go."

"After midnight. So that you were there six hours. Were you given any food during that time?"

"Cup of tea and a sandwich. After I'd made a statement, that was."

"During these six hours were you subjected to lengthy questioning?"

"About half the time, I suppose, maybe a bit more."

Eustace Hardy got up. He looked as though he had smelled something unpleasant. "My lord, I don't see the force of this line of questioning, unless my learned friend is suggesting that the witness was coerced into making his statement."

Newton had not given way. "If I may be permitted to continue, my lord, the relevance of these questions will quickly be apparent."

The Judge looked at them both over his half-lenses.

"Very well, Mr Newton."

Newton raised his voice. "Are you making any complaint at all about being coerced during the questioning?"

There was a painfully long pause. Surely, Newton thought, the young fool's not going to say anything out of line about the police. Then Gardner said in a low voice, "I've got no complaints."

"There is no suggestion that the questioning was anything but perfectly proper. But the point is this, it was a severe and lengthy examination."

"It certainly was."

"How many people questioned you?"

"Sometimes one, mostly two. They changed about."

"Quite so. And how did you feel at the end of it?"

"I was pretty well done for. Just wanted to get to bed."

"You wanted to get to bed," Newton drawled. "And I'm not surprised. Did you have anything to eat when you got home?"

Gardner shook his head. "I went straight to bed. I was out on my feet, ready to drop."

"Did you go out again to Jones's house, and leave a note there?"

"No, I didn't."

"Did you at some time in the small hours go to this place, Platt's Flats, and there take part in an attack on Jones?"

"No." The boy was emphatic. "I was in bed and asleep."

"Right." Newton suddenly became very brisk. "Exhibit 31, please." Exhibit 31 was the pair of grey trousers with the mixture of coal and sand in the turn-ups, upon which so much reliance had been placed. "I want you to look at these trousers." Gardner looked at them, and nodded. "You have heard it suggested that you wore these trousers on Friday night. Is that correct?

"No. I never went out."

"Very good. Now, it is also suggested that these were the trousers that came back from the Kwick-N-Clean laundry on that Friday afternoon. Is that correct?"

"No, it's not."

"How can you be sure?"

"Because I took these trousers to the cleaners myself, and collected them."

"What was the name of the cleaners?"

"Coburg Cleaning. In the High Street."

"And on what date did you collect them?"

The pale figure in the box replied, with no apparent awareness of the shock his words brought, "On Wednesday, the fourteenth of October."

Newton pressed forward, now relentlessly. "How can you be sure of the date?"

"I kept the receipt."

Newton fumbled in front of him, and produced a slip of white paper. "This is the receipt, my lord. I ask that it may be labelled and admitted as an exhibit."

Mr Justice Beckles looked at the slip of paper. "Very well."

There was a good deal of bustling about at the table where the exhibits lay. Then the usher said, "This is Exhibit No.39."

"Thank you. Perhaps the jury would like to look at it."

The piece of paper was passed solemnly round the jury box. It went to Eustace Hardy who glanced at it, his face expressionless, then back to Newton.

"How can you be certain that these are the trousers you took to Coburg Cleaning?"

"They are gaberdine trousers."

"Ah yes. It says so on the receipt, does it not?" He held the receipt at arm's length almost, and read in a loud voice, "'One pair of *gaberdine* trousers, cleaned and pressed.' Is there any special reason why you should remember this pair of gaberdine trousers?"

"Yes. Coburg Cleaning have got a special process they use for gaberdine trousers, supposed to preserve them or something. They told me about it when I took them in. They'd been to Kwick-N-Clean before, and they didn't do them well." Gardner's voice had in it the finicky tone of the smart dresser. He was now almost objectionably at ease.

"You got these trousers back on October the fourteenth. Between that time and November the fifth, did you visit Platt's Flats?"

"Oh yes. It was our meeting-place."

"Did you wear these trousers when you went there?"

"Three or four times, yes."

"Did you go in by the back entrance?"

"Yes, I always did. And a couple of times I stumbled over the old sandpit."

It was time for the finishing stroke. Newton established that Leslie Gardner had only one pair of gaberdine trousers, and then produced and offered as an exhibit a pair of grey worsted trousers, cleaned and pressed and obviously unworn, and suggested that these were the trousers that had gone to the Kwick-N-Clean laundry. Later he was to put into the box a girl from Coburg Cleaning who remembered a conversation with Gardner about the special process for gaberdine trousers, but that merely emphasised the rout of a defeated enemy.

Of the defeat there could be no question. Even those least sensitive to the temper of a court could feel the change in atmosphere, the jauntiness of Newton, and the confidence almost visibly pumped into Leslie Gardner, so that one expected to see his pale cheeks colour and fill out. Little of this was new to Hugh Bennett. He and Fairfield had followed the trail carefully from the moment that they realised the significance of the two pairs of trousers mentioned by Jill, they had presented the evidence to the defence solicitor, George Earl, they had waited for Newton to spring his trap. Now, sitting in court two rows behind and to the side of Jill, Hugh watched her profile, snub-nosed, short-lipped, as she bent forward to take in every nuance of what was happening. Her father, in the next seat, sat with his head slightly bowed, almost as though he were sleeping. Occasionally the head jerked up, the lips moved soundlessly. At times it seemed that he might burst out into laughter.

On the reporters' bench Michael Baker listened, absorbed. "So that was it," he whispered to Fairfield. "Two pairs of trousers."

"Two pairs of trousers."

"And they didn't bother to check."

"They were too sure of themselves. And they didn't want to approach the Gardners, afraid they'd queer the pitch somehow."

203

"My word." Michael breathed it with awe. "Somebody's going to get a rocket."

When the full extent of the catastrophe was realised there was a flurry of agitated movement on the prosecution side. This flurry might have been imperceptible to the untrained eye. It was a matter of papers being turned over in search of something that was not there, wigs brushing together, eyebrows being raised as words were urgently whispered. All this, the wigs in their brushing suggested, was something that they might just possibly, if they had been really *intensely* curious, have thought of questioning, but at the same time it was not their parts to check those lowly details about this pair and that pair of trousers. That was, or at least should be, the work of the police. And Twicker, certainly, was not one to deny this responsibility. The superintendent sat during this evidence with his arms folded, staring straight in front of him. Just once he turned and looked at Norman, and the sick feeling the sergeant had in his stomach was accentuated by the despair and the defeated pride that he saw in Twicker's eyes. It was not fair, Norman wanted to say, it was utterly unfair that the defence should be allowed to work a fiddle like this, and if he had been asked to specify in what exactly the fiddle consisted he would have said that it was quite wrong for the defence to have a chance of springing a surprise like this when the prosecution had had to reveal its own case in advance. As for his part in it, Norman was unrepentant. You didn't get this sort of information by asking an accused man's relatives for it. They had just been unlucky, or a fiddle had been worked on them, that was all.

The person who seemed least moved by this evidence was Eustace Hardy. It was one of Hardy's gifts that he was able to accept such a reverse as this one with extraordinary resilience. To build one's case quite deliberately upon a particular point of strength, and then to find the props utterly sheared away from the attack so carefully mounted, would have demoralised many a lesser man. But Hardy listened to the evidence as Newton took it forward step by step; acknowledged, in his almost impartial way, the cleverness with which the bomb had been timed, and Newton's ingenuity in refraining from embarrassing Twicker or Norman by questions which might have precipitated his surprise too soon; satisfied himself that it was really useless to pursue this aspect of the case any further; and then set himself to find some other chinks in the armour that Newton had put round the frail figure in the dock. When he rose to face an over-confident Leslie Gardner, Hardy's manner had lost nothing of its usual supercilious assurance, his silver voice had a delicacy as tangible as the ring of good glass. Yet the four words of his first question, asked with careless ease, brought Leslie Gardner up with a jolt, the sort of jolt experienced by somebody who, making his way in darkness about the known contours of a room, finds himself stopped by a table or chair in an unaccustomed place.

"Do you like Garney?"

That was the question. Leslie Gardner did not answer it, but stared at the man whose natural elegance he half-consciously recognised and envied, and fingered his tie. Hardy repeated the question. Mr Justice Beckles looked inquiringly, finally spoke.

"Did you hear what counsel asked you?"

"Yes."

"Then you must reply."

Gardner looked at the dark boy in the dock, but there was nothing responsive, nothing that gave a clue to his feelings one way or the other, in King Garney's face.

"Yes," Gardner said, and cleared his throat. "I like him all right."

"Do you like him more than you like the others in your group, or gang, or whatever we are to call it?"

"Yes, I s'pose so."

"What do you mean by 'suppose so'? You know it really, don't you? You like him more than the others?"

"What if I do?"

"I am not saying there was anything wrong about your liking him. But it is right that you do like him, isn't it?"

"Yes," Gardner said abruptly. It looked as though he might burst into tears.

It was just at this moment that Hugh Bennett saw on George Gardner's face, two rows in front of him, a look of eagerness and longing, as though he were waiting for some words that would resolve for him a question he had been waiting half a lifetime to hear answered.

"Your mother is dead, isn't she?" the silver voice went on. "Who has more influence on you, Garney or your father?"

This time there was no doubt of the violence of the reaction. "I don't take any notice of what Dad says."

Was it worth going down this side track? Hardy decided that it was. "Indeed? You go your own way, do you?"

There was something almost pathetic about the defiance with which Gardner said that he did what he wanted, pathetic because he was a boy so obviously destined to take ideas and wishes second-hand, so plainly one whose dreams were synthetic, distorted echoes of something he had heard at a cinema or on a long-playing record.

"Did your father try to influence you?"

The boy said something in a low voice. He did not look at his father.

"What was that?" the Judge squeaked sharply. "Speak up."

"He was always preaching," Gardner said loudly enough, too loudly. "Going on about the workers and that. He never left me alone."

"You resented that?"

"I couldn't stick it. He was always going on."

Jill put her hand on her father's arm. He sat there, staring at his son.

"So you resented your father. You found King Garney more congenial." Hardy knew very well the impression that is always created on a jury by youthful disobedience, and disloyalty to the family. "Is he your best friend?"

"Yes." There was no doubt about it now.

"Do you admire him?"

"Yes," Gardner said boldly. Magnus Newton dug a hole in the paper in front of him with his ball-point pen.

"Enough to do things when he asked you to do them?"

"That would depend."

"Would depend on what he asked?"

"Yes."

"But you were his partner in some of his exploits? He would choose you before any of the others?"

"Yes. We're friends," Leslie Gardner said with fatuous pleasure.

"If Garney had asked you to go up to Platt's Flats with him on that Friday night, would you have gone?"

Too late, the boy saw something of what he had done. "He didn't ask."

"But supposing he had asked," the silvery voice said. "Supposing he had asked you to help him teach Rocky Jones a bit of a lesson, you'd have gone, surely?"

"No, I wouldn't."

"But why not?" Hardy was all silvery surprise. "After all, he was your best friend."

"He never asked me."

"Isn't it true that he said something like that to you, because he knew he could rely on you? And that you went along because you admired him?"

"No. He never asked me."

"And when you got there, you found out that Garney meant to kill Rocky Jones?"

207

"No, it's not true."

"I suggest that you went along with Garney to this disused cottage, and that once there you did what he told you. When you saw that he was going to attack Jones, you helped him. Isn't that the way it happened?"

"No. No." Leslie Gardner looked round the court now for help. He looked at the Judge and at his counsel and at the dark figure of Garney, but he did not look at his father.

Eustace Hardy's voice was incapable of thunderous tones, but Gardner trembled as he heard it, shivered as though he heard a knife scraped across iron. "There was blood on your jacket. Where did it come from?"

"I don't know. I've said already I don't know."

"You don't know," Hardy said softly. "But you are a boy who cares about his clothes, aren't you? You dress smartly, or try to. Are you saying seriously that you didn't notice the spots of blood on your black zipping jacket? Are you really saying that?"

"I must have cut myself."

"But you don't remember doing it?"

"No."

"Can you show me how you might have cut yourself so that blood could have got on to your zipping jacket high up near the shoulder?"

Newton rose, but the Judge forestalled him.

"Mr Hardy, the witness has already said that he does not know how the spots of blood got on to the jacket. I think you must accept that."

"As your lordship pleases," Hardy said loftily. He had now sketched out a whole new plan of attack, and although he could not hope that those unfortunate trousers would be forgotten, he did his best to take the jury's minds from them by concentration on the blood-stains. The cross-examination lasted no more than three hours, but by the time it had finished Leslie Gardner was in need of all the buttressing that Newton could give him in a re-examination which brought out that no attempt had been made to remove the blood spots, that he never wore the zipping jacket except when on his motorcycle, and that he would have been crazy to use a noisy motorcycle to go out to the cottage after midnight on Friday. Gardner walked back from witness box to dock with his head down. In the dock he looked shyly at the figure by his side. Garney gave him one single sharp approving nod.

After Gardner, there followed the girl from Coburg Cleaning. Hardy asked her no questions. The only other defence witness of importance, the mushroom-growing Morgan, provided one of those pieces of anticlimax with which trials are so often spotted. His assertions that it was too dark for Pickett to have identified anybody were questioned with delicate irony by Hardy, who pointed out that Morgan had been able to recognise Pickett, and that a bonfire customarily cast a good glow round about. But nobody really cared about Morgan. The question of Gardner's identification on Guy Fawkes night now seemed much less important than the jury's weighing of the effect created by the unfortunate prosecution mistake about the trousers against the damage done to Gardner by Hardy's cross-examination.

"What do you think?" Hugh asked Fairfield. The crime reporter was sitting in the Goat with Michael. "What are the chances?"

"For Garney, no chance at all. For Leslie, about fifty-fifty."

"No better than that?" He was dismayed. When they had discovered the facts about the cleaning of the gaberdine trousers it had seemed that an acquittal was certain.

"No. He was bad in the box."

"But they built their case on identifying the trousers."

"Hardy switched it cleverly. He's very good. And Leslie got rattled." Fairfield's manner lacked a shade of his usual urbanity. He seemed depressed. "I've had enough of the bloody case. Let's talk about something else. And drink up. On the *Banner*."

They drank up. Afterwards Hugh took a tram to Paradise Vale. Jill opened the door. Her face was white, unreal as a mask.

"Oh, it's you. Come in."

"What's the matter?"

"It's Dad. I think he's going out of his mind. He said today that we'd have to emigrate to Australia." He was about to say that this might be eccentric, but could hardly be called insane, when she added, "He's going up to London tomorrow."

"To London?"

"Yes, to arrange about the passages. So he says. And he says just the two of us will go, that Leslie's not his son. I wish you'd go up and see him."

"Where is he?"

"In the bedroom. He's taken his supper up." They had been talking in whispers. He put an arm round her, but she pushed him away and repeated, "I wish you'd go up."

The conversion of the first floor, the installation of a bathroom, had allowed only the creation of three tiny boxes. In one of these he found George Gardner, sitting up in bed eating curry and rice, which he spooned up eagerly and mumbled in his mouth. He was wearing pyjamas and the open top showed his chest, covered with a mat of grey hair. He raised the spoon in greeting. He looked perfectly sane.

There were photographs round the walls. A man in a cloth cap addressed bare-headed workers, the same man was seen in a bowling alley holding a tankard and uproariously laughing, and again in a wedding group.

"My dad," Gardner said. "A great man. Branch secretary of the miners. I'm the third on the right in that one, with my collar crooked."

A pretty girl, resembling Jill, but with less character in her face, looked out in a cabinet portrait.

"Is that – "

"The wife," Gardner said unclearly, his mouth full of curry.

"Jill looks like her." Gardner did not reply. "I hear you're thinking of going to Australia."

"Soon as we can. I'm going up to London tomorrow to fix things up."

"What about Leslie? The trial, I mean."

"Nothing to do with me. I can't help what happens." He ate another spoonful of curry. "You get to wondering why you do it."

"What do you mean?"

"The whole thing. Your whole life. My dad brought me up in the movement, same way I've brought up Leslie. Used to ride me on his shoulder to meetings when I was a kid. When I was twelve I addressed a thousand envelopes in a day. And went to protest meetings. I've been doing it ever since."

"Yes."

"But why? What's it all for? I'll tell you something." He leaned forward and a few grains of curry-stained rice spilled on to the sheet. "He's not my boy."

At first Hugh did not understand the backward gesture made towards a small modern chest of drawers. Then he saw the schoolboy with cap on, neat and pertly smiling. "That's Leslie?"

"He's not my boy. I told you I brought him up the same way I was brought up myself. No boy of mine would be a Ted, a little whimpering hooligan who – " He began to shout obscenities.

"He's been led away." How feeble the words were. But what other words, what powerful words, could one use?

"He's not mine." The man in the bed began to talk about his wife, and recounted to Hugh's appalled ears her sexual habits, describing in detail the men she had been with and the times he had found her with them and saying it all with a ghastly relish that was almost unendurable. Once or twice Hugh tried to break in, to expostulate, but the obscenities went resistlessly on. There was still a little curry left on the plate, and when Gardner stopped and began to eat it, Hugh opened the door.

Downstairs Jill asked, "What did he say?" He did not know how to reply. "Was it about my mother?"

"Some of it."

"It isn't true, you know that, don't you? They were wonderfully happy with each other, devoted. Mum never looked at anybody else." She pressed herself close against him. Her body quivered, but she did not cry. "What am I to do?"

"Perhaps you ought to get a doctor. But most of the time he seemed all right, a bit odd, that's all."

"I'm afraid calling in a doctor will make him worse. The real thing is that he thinks Leslie will be found guilty. He was bad in the box, wasn't he? But that doesn't mean anything."

She made a pot of tea and they sat in the kitchen and talked for an hour, talked in the haphazard way of lovers, finding satisfaction in the mere exchange of glances and touch of hands. There was no sound from upstairs.

Chapter Forty-one

The letter came the following morning. It was written on the thick paper used by *Banner* executives, printed in elephant type, and signed by Edgar Crawley, Editor. Like most important letters from newspapers, it was short. It said:

Dear Mr Bennett,
   I have read your contributions about the Guy Fawkes murder with great interest, and have heard a lot about you from Frank Fairfield. If you will let me know when you are next in London, we can have a chat together over a bite of lunch.

Michael read the few lines over and over again, spellbound, and let the toast burn. "Boy," he said, "oh, boy, you've done it. You really have done it. I'd never have believed it possible."

"I haven't done anything yet. I mean, nothing has been offered."

"It will be. Don't you like that bite of lunch? He'd never suggest a bite of lunch unless there was a job going with it." Michael wiped away an imaginary tear and declaimed perverted Christina Rossetti. "Remember me when you are gone away, gone far away into the noisy land. If there's a job going for a junior assistant to the assistant dramatic critic, remember me."

"I'm not sure I want to go."

"Don't let's have any of that. This is the sort of chance that you only get once in a lifetime, if that. You really stepped into the horse manure that night in Far Wether. Just allow fertilisation to proceed according to nature, as Farmer Giles would say."

"Don't tell anybody about it."

"I'll be silent as the third murderer. But I don't see what stops you sitting down and writing a letter now."

"I want to think about it. You don't think they're paying me off for changing my evidence?"

"Don't be crazy."

Looking at the long, weak, handsome face that smiled at him enthusiastically across the breakfast table, Hugh said, "Thank you for everything, Michael."

"Nothing to thank me for. I'm jealous as hell, and I shall make all sorts of catty remarks about you when you've gone. But it's plain as the nose on King Solomon's face that you ought to go. Send a telegram."

What happened at the office seemed to reinforce Michael's words. Lane greeted him with a grin of pure delighted malice, and sent him out first to interview a man who had escaped with minor bruises from a lift which crashed down four floors to a basement, and then to see the new plane launched by the city's flying club and to interview the club's president. It took a long time to get the plane into the air, the club president was very loquacious, and when Hugh was sent afterwards into the suburb of Natley to see a man who claimed to have the biggest collection of outdoor cacti in the country, he felt inclined to take Michael's advice and send a telegram.

"Variety," Lane said, showing his yellow teeth. "It's the spice of life, young feller me lad. Later on you'll thank me, you'll say he was a tough old so and so but he gave me an education in journalism."

"Shall I?" Hugh snatched the piece of paper with the cacti grower's address on it.

Lane rolled a cigar round in his mouth and said in mock-affected tones, "I say, I'm awfully sorry you're missing the end of that trial. I'm sure Newton's making a perfectly magnificent closing speech. Hard cheese, young Bennett."

So it was that Hugh Bennett did not hear what was said afterwards to have been one of Magnus Newton's best performances, or Eustace Hardy's beautifully clear demonstration of the two boys' guilt, or Mr Justice Beckles' tedious but impeccable summing up. The cacti grower also was expansive, pressing upon him a variety of seeds, launching into great bursts of speech about his favourite plants and finally, when Hugh had made far more notes than he would ever use and thought his tribulation over, revealing a whole further group of succulents sprouting away in a roof garden. It was just four o'clock when he got back to the city, nearly ten past when he saw the crowd outside the Assize Court and heard the noise that they were making, a noise that was not precisely cheering but had some unidentifiable quality about it, a sort of baying pleasure. He got off his tram and began to run.

A woman with a shopping basket appeared in his path. Swerving to avoid her, he struck the basket. Vegetables shot out into the road. "Sorry," he gasped, "sorry, sorry," as he knelt down and threw them in again, all the time feeling the people swaying like a cloud of bees, feeling a desperately important need to be with them, asking questions that nobody seemed to answer. At last the potatoes and endless sprouts, the apples and biscuits were back in the basket and he was moving in a jog-trot walk towards the crowd and was positively in it, saying, "What has happened? What's the verdict?" and getting only a confused roar for reply. He clutched the arm of a woman so fat that she looked as though breasts, stomach, buttocks, were separate inflated balloons.

His fingers sunk into the arm, he felt that he might by mistake prick her so that she collapsed with a sigh. Instead she turned, swung the other arm, and slapped his face with a meaty palm, crying "Take your hands off me."

He took away the hand, stammered something. Her great flanks struck against him as she moved away. He said loudly to a small anxious-looking man with a toothbrush moustache, "What happened?"

"Don't ask me."

"But weren't you in court?"

The little man wore a raincoat much too long for him. The sleeves came down so far that you could not see his hands. "Not me. I was just – "

He never learned what the little man had been doing, for a gentle movement in the crowd shifted its pattern, as the pieces in a kaleidoscope change when the tube is shaken. In the re-formed pattern Hugh saw tantalisingly near to him the long face and the enveloping blue duffle coat of the mushroom-farmer, Morgan. Another susurration in the crowd and they were side by side. "Morgan," he cried, "Morgan."

"Hallo. Let's get out of this and have a drink."

"What happened?"

"Have a drink."

"The pubs are shut."

"I know a place." Morgan leered at him, unnaturally gay.

They were drifting apart. "I wasn't in court," he called. "Don't know the result."

"Gardner acquitted, Garney guilty," Morgan shouted. "Too clever for his own good, that Hardy. The Ace of Spades in Clough Street, see you there."

Hugh pushed and used his elbows, and suddenly was out of the crowd. Like a swimmer coming up from under water he looked at the men and women now slowly dispersing, and saw that there were not so many of them, after all. A

216

hundred, perhaps? Certainly not more. And now that he came to listen to them, his diver's ears unstopped, he heard fragmentary phrases about Gardner, how lucky he had been and what a flimsy case it was against him and how wrong it was that he should ever have been charged. Had people been saying these things all the time?

In the High Street he got a taxi. On the way out to Paradise Vale he examined his own feelings, and was surprised to find not exhilaration but a sort of numbness in his mind. It was all over, they had won, and he was conscious only of emptiness. It was as though the trial had become for him normality, and the end of it signified not victory or defeat, but some terrible change impending in his own life.

The taxi drew up short of the Gardners' house in Peter Street. The driver said, "Quite a party."

Hugh stood staring. Half a dozen cars were drawn up beside or near to the house, and a number of people moved about the gate, some of them with cameras. The door opened, and with a shock he recognised the trim figure and neat fair head of Sally Banstead. He heard her voice, clear and slightly shrill. "You might just as well give up, boys. Leslie's too tired to talk."

"Let him say so himself," somebody called. Another voice said, "Can it, Sally."

Sally hesitated, then said, "All right. He'll come out. But just pictures, that's all. He really is tired."

Now Leslie Gardner himself appeared in the doorway, with Sally on one side of him and Frank Fairfield on the other. Half a dozen cameras were raised. There was no expression at all on Leslie Gardner's face. A patter of questions rained down.

"How does it feel to be acquitted?"

"Were you ever worried, Leslie?"

"What are your plans now?"

"What do you think about your counsel, Mr Newton?"

"Who found out about the second pair of trousers?"

Leslie Gardner stood in the doorway, swaying on his feet a little, and said nothing at all. Sally Banstead put a hand on his shoulder, whispered something, and stepped forward. "He can't answer questions, boys, you can see that, he's too tired. You've got your pictures."

"So be good boys and go away," somebody said. There was general laughter. Hugh pushed his way to the gate as the three figures were going in. "Frank," he called. Fairfield turned, waved, held the door open.

He was in the dark narrow passage, with Fairfield beside him and Sally facing them. Sally's lip was drawn back in a snarl. She spoke in a ferocious whisper.

"Who are you? Oh, I know, the boy from the local paper. Is he all right?"

"Of course," Fairfield said.

"How am I to know, the way you've fixed it? Why bring them here at all, why couldn't we go to a hotel?"

Fairfield's voice, equally low, was elaborately patient. "Sally dear, they wouldn't go to a hotel, they wouldn't come anywhere but here."

"We paid for the defence, didn't we? What goes on?"

"If you'll just wait, you'll find it works out this way."

"And what's wrong with them? The way they're behaving, you'd think they'd sooner he'd been found guilty."

"Perhaps it would have been simpler," Fairfield said.

"I don't know what you mean." In the dark passage he could sense Sally's almost physical irritation. "Oh well, let's go in and have another try."

In the small sitting-room Jill and her father sat together on the red moquette sofa. Jill's hands were folded on her lap, her face was pale. George Gardner stared straight across the room at the Van Gogh self-portrait. He did not turn his head as they came in. The thought passed through Hugh's mind that George Gardner hadn't after all, gone to London, and he

218

wondered briefly whether the whole thing last night had been some kind of act put on for their benefit. Then he looked at Leslie, who sat in one of the armchairs, perfectly still except that his fingers drummed continuously on its arm. The fourth person in the room was a sports-jacketed photographer, who had put down camera and flash, and stood leaning against the wall looking bored. Into this silent and hostile tableau Sally Banstead crisply stepped. Beside her bright vitality Jill looked slightly washed out, and the stillness of Leslie and his father seemed somehow slightly ridiculous. She stood with her back to the ornamental fireplace.

"That's got rid of them. For the moment, anyway. You were fine, Leslie. Now, let's get on. Can we just have a family group first?"

"We don't want any photographs. I just told you." George Gardner said it a little unclearly, but with heavy decision.

"Come along now. You made an arrangement with the *Banner*. It's up to you to keep it."

Leslie stopped drumming. "I never made an arrangement."

_ "You knew Magnus Newton was going to defend you. The whole thing was explained to you."

"I never made an arrangement. I never signed anything."

Sally took a cigarette out of a small jewelled case, snapped a smaller jewelled lighter. The surface pleasantness of her voice was rubbing away. "What is it you want? More money?"

"We don't want any of your bloody money," George Gardner said. His lack of teeth turned *bloody* into *bluthy*.

Sally puffed twice at the cigarette, then stubbed it out into an ashtray shaped like a horse. "Frank, you take over." She went across and stood beside the photographer.

Fairfield had been smoking, too. Now he put down his cigarette on the edge of another ashtray, this one shaped like a bear with one claw clutching the cigarette, and began to talk in a low voice, as though he were rehearsing arguments which they already knew by heart.

"I don't know why we're not all out in a pub having a drink. That's where I should like to be. It's a sort of let-down after all this time to be sitting here arguing, instead of celebrating."

"I don't feel like celebrating," George Gardner said.

Fairfield ignored him. "But let's get this straight. And let's keep a sense of proportion. You don't love the *Banner*, don't want anything more to do with it. All right. But you ought to face this. Without young Hugh here and me digging around and finding out about the trousers, which was something Leslie himself didn't remember until he was questioned, perhaps he wouldn't have been acquitted. Without Newton to defend him he might not have got off. You've got a contract with the *Banner* – "

"Let them sue," George Gardner said. It sounded like *shoe.*"

"You think they won't sue. And you're probably right. But it doesn't end with the contract. Whether you like the *Banner* or not, you owe them just about the biggest debt any family could owe to a newspaper. Probably you can get out of paying it. But I know what sort of names Mr Gardner here would use for a trade unionist who tried to welsh on that sort of a debt."

Fairfield picked up his cigarette. His hand was shaking badly. Jill moved on the sofa, as though breaking a spell. "He's right. You both know it." They said nothing. Like a general settling the terms of surrender after a defeat, she said to Fairfield, "What exactly do you want?"

They had been over all this before, as Hugh Bennett sensed. "Photographs first. Some of Leslie, one or two groups. After all, the other papers have got them, you wouldn't want the *Banner* to be treated worse than the others, I hope. Then Leslie and I go out together, spend the night in some quiet hotel, have dinner, rough out his story. We shall want three articles, four if it seems to run to that."

"You're going to write it for him," George Gardner said.

"That just isn't true." Fairfield's weary patience seemed to be endless. "Leslie can't write the story himself. There's a form it's got to go in, a way people like to read things in a newspaper. This is going to be Leslie's story, though, I'm not going to invent anything. It's going to be the story of his life, childhood, family, schooling, everything that led up to the trial, then the trial itself and his feelings while it was going on, and when he heard the verdict. As straightforward as that."

"Why has it got to be tonight?" That was Jill. "Let him have twenty-four hours. He needs a rest."

Fairfield shook his head. "Tonight. We're late on it already. We just can't afford to leave it for another day."

To nobody in particular, Jill said, "We do owe it to them."

There was silence. Then Sally Banstead made a gesture to the photographer. Like actors who have been waiting impatiently in the wings, they moved into the middle of the room. "Is the chair all right?" Sally said.

"One in the chair, then standing, then a group."

"What about boyish treasures?" The words sounded odd on Sally's lips. "Cricket bats, football boots you used when you got a hat-trick for the first team, cup you won for running, you know the sort of thing. Sounds corny, but people like it."

Leslie Gardner stirred in his chair. He did not look at Sally, but spoke to Fairfield. "What about King?"

"King?"

"In this story of yours. What about King? Where does he come in?"

For the first time that evening Fairfield seemed taken aback, although he answered easily enough. "We'll have to

221

talk that over. Of course you'll have to say something about King."

"They found him guilty. Is he going to hang?"

Again he spoke to Fairfield directly, as though only from Fairfield could he expect the truth.

"It's possible, Leslie. He's nineteen years old."

"They wouldn't have hung me?"

"That's right. You're only seventeen."

"Oh, come on. Let's get on with it." Sally made a gesture. There was a flash of light, momentarily startling. The photographer said something like, "Another one, I think, standing this time." But Hugh could not hear the words distinctly because Leslie Gardner, his face white as milk, was standing up and shouting at them.

"Then why don't they hang me? I don't want to be let off. I was in it too, wasn't I?"

Jill was on her feet. Hugh never forgot the expressions on their faces, the open-mouthed surprise of Sally Banstead, the questing pleasure in the photographer's stare, the dismay of Fairfield, the hand that Jill put up as though to ward off an advancing figure in a nightmare. Only George Gardner sat apparently unmoved, his stiff collar tight round his neck, his arms straining at the cloth of the suit he wore. And it was George Gardner who said to his son, in the voice thickened and made ridiculous by the lack of teeth, "What do you mean?"

"I was there. That's what I mean. I was there. You all know it, don't you?"

"No." Fairfield's voice was for once loudly emphatic. "We don't know anything. Don't say it, Leslie."

The boy took no notice. He was talking now to his father. "I was in it, right up to here. Because King asked me to, that's why. I'd do anything for King, you know that, don't you, anything he asked. You knew it all the time. Didn't you? Didn't you? Eh?" He said this while Fairfield was shouting at the top of his voice *shut up, shut up,* said it as though there were only two people in the room.

"The trousers," Jill said. "What about the trousers?"

"I wore my old brown suit, of course, factory clothes." Now he looked round at the rest of them. "Doesn't matter what I say now, does it? I've been let off, they can't do a bloody thing about it."

Sally Banstead said under her breath, wonderingly almost, "That's torn it, that's really torn it."

Leslie was staring at his father again. His lips were trembling, his eyes were melting with tears. He repeated softly, "You knew it, Dad, didn't you?"

George Gardner stood up. He looked at his son's trembling lips and imploring eyes. Then he gathered saliva in his mouth. The spittle landed on Leslie's cheek. The boy began to cry.

"Oh, Dad," he said, and kept repeating it. "Oh, Dad."

"A nancy boy and a murderer," Gardner said. "Not my son." As he walked past Leslie, the boy clung to his jacket. Without visible effort Gardner turned and struck him. It was not a hard blow, but a ring on his finger cut the boy's mouth. Gardner walked out of the room. They heard the front door slam.

"Frank," Sally Banstead said. She looked more nearly human than Hugh had seen her. Fairfield nodded. They went out with the photographer.

"That's the end of it," Jill said. She looked down at Leslie, who now crouched on the floor, making snuffling noises.

"Is there anything I can do?" He felt the absurdity of the question, the inadequacy of any words.

"Go away, Hugh. I want everyone to go away."

"Will you come too?"

"How can I? He's my brother." She rested a hand on Leslie's head. He did not look up.

Hugh went away and walked through the streets of Paradise Vale. It seemed long afterwards, but perhaps it was little more than an hour, when he walked into the American Bar of the Grand. Fairfield sat on a stool there, with Sally Banstead by his side. Fairfield raised a hand in greeting, and began to talk.

"You are just in time to take part in a top-level conference, a council of war. Shall we let young Hugh in on our conference, Sally?" Sally stared at him with her bright shallow eyes, but said nothing. "Sally and I are trying to work out a plan. Sally has been revealing the unsuspected presence of a heart, and I have been using the gin-soaked thing that passes for my brain. We have decided that if young Leslie could be parted from his family it would be a good thing for everybody. Young Leslie included. Agreed?"

Fairfield was not drunk, he could never be drunk, but there was something odd about the vague eyes behind the thick glasses.

Hugh said stupidly, "I don't know. But what's it got to do with you?"

"There's a little matter of a life-story being written," Sally said. "Perhaps it escaped you."

"But you can't do that. Not after what he said."

"Why not?" She snapped open her bag, looked at her face in a square of glass.

"But you heard what he said. You can't do it, you simply can't do it."

The face passed inspection, the bag was shut. "What you can't do you have to do sometimes."

"Frank," he said to Fairfield.

"Look at it Sally's way, and that's one answer. The paper's paid for its story, and it's got to have it. But look at it another way. Leslie was hysterical this afternoon, didn't know what he was saying. He said it to spite his father, couldn't you feel it? He'd have said anything to make his father react in the way he did."

"I like Sally's answer."

"Look at it another way. Do you remember what I said to you once? You play the game according to the rules. There's no other way to play it. When you lose you don't cry, and when you have a lucky win you don't ask questions."

"I still like Sally's answer. The paper's paid its money and you've got to give them a story. Isn't that right?"

Fairfield looked at him for a long moment, and then said almost indifferently, "If you like."

They had bought him a drink, and it was in his hand. It seemed that there was a great distance between his hand and the bar counter, so that the glass came down heavily, and some of the drink spilled over. He looked once at Fairfield and seemed to see for the first time that what stood at the bar was hardly more than the wreck of a human being, a wreck staying afloat on its sea of drink. Then he turned his back, and again it seemed to be a long way from the bar to the door.

Michael was in the flat, cooking bacon and eggs. "Our boy won," he said.

"Yes."

"You don't look very pleased. Old Beckles summed up dead in his favour, pointed out how thin it all was really, highly circumstantial. But the boob about the trousers did the trick, if you ask me. Have you sent that telegram?"

"What telegram? No, I haven't." He took Crawley's letter out of his pocket and tore it into small pieces. Then he walked to the lavatory, put the pieces in the pan and pulled the chain. Michael, who had followed him, stood in admiration.

"Do you know, I've often heard about people doing that, but I've never seen it done." He went back to his bacon and eggs and said reflectively, "But still, you can always send the telegram."

Chapter Forty-two

When the case was over Magnus Newton posed, beaming, for photographs, said thank you to Toby Bander, exchanged congratulations with Charles Earl, and went back as quickly as he could to Hampton Court. He greeted his wife by flapping his arms and crowing like a cock, and this did not surprise her because it was his custom when particularly elated. They ate a very simple meal – an omelette and salad, with a bottle of Pol Roget – and then he talked about the case until his wife fell asleep.

Eustace Hardy travelled back to London by the same train, but not in the same carriage. He felt very little emotion about Leslie Gardner's acquittal, but found Newton brash, vulgar, and generally antipathetic. Hardy spent the evening in the club, where nobody talked to him about the case. He played three rubbers of bridge, which he considered the only card game worthy of serious intellectual concentration, and then read Macaulay in bed.

Twicker and Norman were also on the train. They sat opposite each other, but hardly spoke. On the following morning Twicker's letter of resignation was on the AC's desk. Acceptance of the resignation at that time would have been an acknowledgement that the case had been badly handled. The AC sent for Twicker, talked to him for half an hour, and tore up the letter. Twicker was never again trusted with an investigation of any importance. Twelve months later he wrote another letter of resignation, and this time it was accepted.

Nothing happened to Norman, beyond a verbal barrage from which he emerged much shaken. In such matters the sins of sergeants are often visited upon superintendents, and within a few months Norman was as cockily ebullient as ever. On the rare occasions when he saw Twicker he was greeted with a nod. The two men never worked together again.

When he left his house George Gardner went round to his closest political associate, a man named Carpenter, and told him that he had changed his mind about giving up politics and leaving the district. He was going to stay and fight it out. Gardner's lack of teeth made the militancy of his speech sound comic, but he did not seem comic to Carpenter. The two men sat talking together until after three o'clock in the morning.

Garney went back to his cell. His warders saw no diminution of the hard indifferent courage he had shown during his trial.

Jill Gardner tried to talk to her brother, and made a pot of tea and some sandwiches. He would neither eat nor drink, nor would he speak to her. At nine o'clock he went up to his room. Half an hour later she went to bed, and fell asleep almost immediately.

Leslie Gardner did not sleep. Perhaps he spent the time until midnight thinking about Garney, or perhaps he was awaiting his father's return. It must have been at about midnight, the doctor said afterwards, that he knotted his braces, tied them to the hook on the back of his bedroom door, stood on a chair, put his head through the noose, pulled it tight, and kicked away the chair. George Gardner found him when he came home at half-past three, and saw a light on in his son's room.

Chapter Forty-three

Fairfield heard the news on his hotel bedroom radio at nine o'clock on the following morning, while he was shaving. His hand was shaking very badly, and he felt even worse than he usually felt at this time of day. He cut himself, staunched the bleeding, finished shaving, and then telephoned Crawley at his home. By ten-thirty he and Sally Banstead and the photographer were on their way back to London. At the office Fairfield asked for and obtained three days' leave. He went on a forty-eight-hour drinking jag that ended in a fight with a sailor. In the fight he suffered a black eye and his glasses were broken. He spent a day on soda water and biscuits and turned up in the office at the end of his leave with a black patch over the eye and wearing a spare pair of glasses, but otherwise little the worse for wear.

Crawley telephoned the news to Lord Brackman.

"I see." Lord Brackman's breathing sounded more than usually thick, there was the preliminary throat-clearing, and then one word. "Why?"

"I don't know. And it's better not to guess. I've told Frank and Sally to come back."

Such an acknowledgement by Crawley that he had assumed authority was so rare that it gave Lord Brackman pause. "Yes," he said after a while. "Kill it, Edgar. Kill it."

"We shall have to say something about the suicide."

"A paragraph." Another pause. "Had Fairfield got any of the story?"

"Not yet. Things were awkward, from what I gather. There were family complications."

"I don't want to hear any more." The thick voice choked up, and then began to whine. "I don't want to argue about this."

Crawley said crisply, "One more thing. We were going to pay for the story. But there's no story. I don't feel that there's any need – "

"I leave it to you, I've got every faith in you. No unpleasantness, that's the thing. No argument. And, Edgar."

"Yes, Brack?"

"Send a wreath."

Hugh heard the news from Clare when he went into the office at about half-past ten. She handed him the message as it had come through on the tape, without saying anything. Then she said, "Lane's out. But somebody will have to handle it. I don't suppose you want to do it, Hugh. If I were you – "

He did not wait for the end of the sentence. It was raining heavily out of a leaden sky as he walked down Peter Street. The blinds of the house were drawn, but Jill saw him, and opened the door. She took him into the kitchen. She was composed, dry-eyed.

"This really is the end of it," she said. "Poor Leslie."

"Poor Leslie."

Feet sounded on the stairs. Before he had time to ask how her father had taken it, George Gardner appeared in the doorway. He looked tired but cheerful. "Hallo, young Hugh. Is there a pot of tea, Jill?"

"I've got the kettle on." She was at the gas cooker and now, without turning, she said, "Dad's staying on."

"You've got to fight it out." Gardner nodded at Hugh. "No use running away from things. I settled that last night, talking to Charlie Carpenter. That was before I came back and found him. That was his trouble, running away from things."

"Leslie?"

"If we'd never let those vultures of the press get at him, he'd have been all right. That was the biggest mistake I ever made. Coming here last night the way they did. The boy didn't know what he was saying. I reckon they drove him to it." So that was to be the way of it, Hugh thought incredulously, like Fairfield last night Gardner was to maintain that Leslie's words had not borne their plain and obvious meaning. "He was a victim," Gardner said now in a voice that might have been impressive but for its tooth-lacking lisp, "a victim of the capitalist press."

The kettle shrieked. Jill poured water in the pot. "Dad's staying on, but I'm going."

Hugh stared at her. "Where to?"

"I don't know. Out of Peter Street. And out of my job. It's now or never. I know what I'm like."

Gardner said cheerfully, "Charlie Carpenter's got a spare room that would just about suit me. He was talking about it last night as a matter of fact. And I shouldn't want to stay on after – " He nodded upwards. He couldn't have endured his son alive, Hugh thought, but he's a useful symbol now that he's dead. They drank the tea, and Gardner looked at his watch. "I think I'll go round and have a word with Charlie now. You'll be all right?" he said to Jill.

"Of course."

"I won't be more than half an hour."

When the door had closed he said, "Jill?"

"Yes."

"I had a letter from the *Banner.* An invitation to lunch."

"Are you going?"

"No. But I'm not staying at the *Gazette* either."

"What are you going to do?"

"I don't know. Do you think two temporarily unemployed people ought to get married?"

"Not when one of them is a meat and two veg girl."

"But you're not. If you were you'd be staying here, staying in your job."

"I can't talk about it. Not in this house."

"Then let's go for a walk. You'd better put on your raincoat. It's pouring."

They went out into the city.

JULIAN SYMONS

THE BROKEN PENNY

An Eastern-bloc country, shaped like a broken penny, was being torn apart by warring resistance movements. Only one man could unite the hostile factions – Professor Jacob Arbitzer. Arbitzer, smuggled into the country by Charles Garden during the Second World War, has risen to become president, only to have to be smuggled out again when the communists gained control. Under pressure from the British Government who want him reinstated, Arbitzer agreed to return on one condition – that Charles Garden again escort him. *The Broken Penny* is a thrilling spy adventure brilliantly recreating the chilling conditions of the Cold War.

'Thrills, horrors, tears and irony'
– *Times Literary Supplement*

'The most exciting, astonishing and believable spy thriller to appear in years' – *The New York Times*

Julian Symons

The Colour of Murder

John Wilkins was a gentle, mild-mannered man who lived a simple, predictable life. So when he met a beautiful, irresistible girl his world was turned upside down. Looking at his wife, and thinking of the girl, everything turned red before his eyes – the colour of murder. Later, his mind a blank, his only defence was that he loved his wife far too much to hurt her...

'A book to delight every puzzle-suspense enthusiast'
– *The New York Times*

The End of Solomon Grundy

When a girl turns up dead in a Mayfair Mews, the police want to write it off as just another murdered prostitute, but Superintendent Manners isn't quite so sure. He is convinced that the key to the crime lies in The Dell – an affluent suburban housing estate. And in The Dell lives Solomon Grundy. Could he have killed the girl? So Superintendent Manners thinks.

Julian Symons

A Man Called Jones

The office party was in full swing so no one heard the shot – fired at close range through the back of Lionel Hargreaves, elder son of the founder of Hargreaves Advertising Agency. The killer left only one clue – a pair of yellow gloves – but it looked almost as if he had wanted them to be found. As Inspector Bland sets out to solve the murder, he encounters a deadly trail of deception, suspense – and two more dead bodies.

The Players and the Game

'Count Dracula meets Bonnie Parker. What will they do together? The vampire you'd hate to love, sinister and debonair, sinks those eye teeth into Bonnie's succulent throat.'

Is this the beginning of a sadistic relationship or simply an extract from a psychopath's diary? Either way it marks the beginning of a dangerous game that is destined to end in chilling terror and bloody murder.

'Unusual, ingenious and fascinating as a poisonous snake'
– *Sunday Telegraph*

Julian Symons

The Plot Against Roger Rider

Roger Rider and Geoffrey Paradine had known each other since childhood. Roger was the intelligent, good-looking, successful one and Geoffrey was the one everyone else picked on. When years of suppressed anger, jealousy and frustration finally surfaced, Geoffrey took his revenge by sleeping with Roger's beautiful wife. Was this price enough for all those miserable years of putdowns? When Roger turned up dead the police certainly didn't think so.

'[Symons] is in diabolical top form' – *Washington Post*

OTHER TITLES BY JULIAN SYMONS AVAILABLE DIRECT
FROM HOUSE OF STRATUS

Quantity	£	$(US)	$(CAN)	€
CRIME/SUSPENSE				
THE 31ST OF FEBRUARY	6.99	11.50	15.99	11.50
THE BELTING INHERITANCE	6.99	11.50	15.99	11.50
BLAND BEGINNING	6.99	11.50	15.99	11.50
THE BROKEN PENNY	6.99	11.50	15.99	11.50
THE COLOUR OF MURDER	6.99	11.50	15.99	11.50
THE END OF SOLOMON GRUNDY	6.99	11.50	15.99	11.50
THE GIGANTIC SHADOW	6.99	11.50	15.99	11.50
THE IMMATERIAL MURDER CASE	6.99	11.50	15.99	11.50
THE KILLING OF FRANCIE LAKE	6.99	11.50	15.99	11.50
A MAN CALLED JONES	6.99	11.50	15.99	11.50
THE MAN WHO KILLED HIMSELF	6.99	11.50	15.99	11.50
THE MAN WHO LOST HIS WIFE	6.99	11.50	15.99	11.50
THE MAN WHOSE DREAMS CAME TRUE	6.99	11.50	15.99	11.50
THE NARROWING CIRCLE	6.99	11.50	15.99	11.50

ALL HOUSE OF STRATUS BOOKS ARE AVAILABLE FROM GOOD BOOKSHOPS
OR DIRECT FROM THE PUBLISHER:

Internet: www.houseofstratus.com including author interviews, reviews, features.

Email: **sales@houseofstratus.com** please quote author, title and credit card details.

OTHER TITLES BY JULIAN SYMONS AVAILABLE DIRECT
FROM HOUSE OF STRATUS

Quantity		£	$(US)	$(CAN)	€
☐	THE PAPER CHASE	6.99	11.50	15.99	11.50
☐	THE PLAYERS AND THE GAME	6.99	11.50	15.99	11.50
☐	THE PLOT AGAINST ROGER RIDER	6.99	11.50	15.99	11.50
☐	A THREE-PIPE PROBLEM	6.99	11.50	15.99	11.50
	HISTORY/CRITICISM				
☐	BULLER'S CAMPAIGN	8.99	14.99	22.50	15.00
☐	THE TELL-TALE HEART: THE LIFE AND WORKS OF EDGAR ALLEN POE	8.99	14.99	22.50	15.00
☐	ENGLAND'S PRIDE	8.99	14.99	22.50	15.00
☐	THE GENERAL STRIKE	8.99	14.99	22.50	15.00
☐	HORATIO BOTTOMLEY	8.99	14.99	22.50	15.00
☐	THE THIRTIES	8.99	14.99	22.50	15.00
☐	THOMAS CARLYLE	8.99	14.99	22.50	15.00

ALL HOUSE OF STRATUS BOOKS ARE AVAILABLE FROM GOOD BOOKSHOPS
OR DIRECT FROM THE PUBLISHER:

Order Line: UK: 0800 169 1780,
             USA: 1 800 509 9942
             INTERNATIONAL: +44 (0) 20 7494 6400 (UK)
                     or +01 212 218 7649
             (please quote author, title, and credit card details.)

Send to: House of Stratus Sales Department   House of Stratus Inc.
           24c Old Burlington Street   Suite 210
           London   1270 Avenue of the Americas
           W1X 1RL   New York • NY 10020
           UK   USA

PAYMENT

Please tick currency you wish to use:

☐ £ (Sterling)   ☐ $ (US)   ☐ $ (CAN)   ☐ € (Euros)

Allow for shipping costs charged per order plus an amount per book as set out in the tables below:

CURRENCY/DESTINATION

	£(Sterling)	$(US)	$(CAN)	€(Euros)
Cost per order				
UK	1.50	2.25	3.50	2.50
Europe	3.00	4.50	6.75	5.00
North America	3.00	3.50	5.25	5.00
Rest of World	3.00	4.50	6.75	5.00
Additional cost per book				
UK	0.50	0.75	1.15	0.85
Europe	1.00	1.50	2.25	1.70
North America	1.00	1.00	1.50	1.70
Rest of World	1.50	2.25	3.50	3.00

PLEASE SEND CHEQUE OR INTERNATIONAL MONEY ORDER.

payable to: STRATUS HOLDINGS plc or HOUSE OF STRATUS INC. or card payment as indicated

STERLING EXAMPLE

Cost of book(s):..................... Example: 3 x books at £6.99 each: £20.97

Cost of order: .... Example: £1.50 (Delivery to UK address)

Additional cost per book:.............. Example: 3 x £0.50: £1.50

Order total including shipping:........... Example: £23.97

VISA, MASTERCARD, SWITCH, AMEX:

☐☐☐☐☐☐☐☐☐☐☐☐☐☐☐☐☐☐☐☐

Issue number (Switch only):

☐☐☐

Start Date: **Expiry Date:**

☐☐/☐☐   ☐☐/☐☐

Signature: _____

NAME: _____

ADDRESS: _____

COUNTRY: _____

ZIP/POSTCODE: _____

Please allow 28 days for delivery. Despatch normally within 48 hours.

Prices subject to change without notice.
Please tick box if you do not wish to receive any additional information. ☐

House of Stratus publishes many other titles in this genre; please check our website (**www.houseofstratus.com**) for more details.